My Aries...
Secrets

Acknowledgements

My list of acknowledgements in <u>My Scorpio Soul</u> was mainly to my family. This time I want to acknowledge friends and extended family. You are the ones who so looked over my manuscript, hosted launch parties, or came to a book signing. Others of you told friends about my new book series, bought more than one copy to share with friends, requested it on Kindle or wrote a review. I am deeply touched by this support. Still others of you have cheered me on while giving me suggestions. Students drew my cover design and took photos. The list of people I am grateful to would fill pages and pages; but there are a few that absolutely must be mentioned: my mom, Joy, whose name defines her, Gwen, Lori, Sheila, Mariellen, Maria, Kendra, Carol, Monique, Meg, Dr. Nasir, Mary Beth, Teri, Maura, Colleen, Joanne, Mary Pat, Ian, Tekin, Jim Buckley, Ami, Cousins Carol, Susan and Margaret, Karna, Hillary, Marissa, Lenore, Cynthia, Carole Ann, and Chella... thank you to each and every single one of you. And, most especially, I thank my family: Shauna, Kevin, Casey, and Paul for being so patient with me when I am so involved in my writing.

Claudia Hoag Mc Garry

ARIES, the first sign of the zodiac, symbolizes a new beginning. An Aries hates weakness. She is the sign of the eternal warrior. The Aries element is fire. An Aries woman can do something strong and is often impulsive. However, she will also be creative. For example, she may use a kitchen tool or an acrylic painting tool for her killing needs. If the victim doesn't fight back, she will despise this person even more.

Do not think for one moment you can break an Aries woman.

She has no breaking point.

Prologue

HAVEN WROTE TO ME

By: *Tempest Mc Tierney*

I have been thinking about our secrets. The secrets we each keep deep inside ourselves about desire, regret, fear, and love. The cacophony of voices we can hear inside of our heads all day, everyday. No one else hears them. I hear silence eventually comes out. Truth escapes into the air. Does that mean our secrets are eventually told?

This night I tossed and turned until I finally fell asleep picturing Peter standing beside me, watching the Maui sunset, with my many secrets churning inside my head. Then, as I drifted off, in my darkest dream, a woman's voice reached me in the same sleep and she whispered into my ear:

"I can do this. Me, Haven Rodriquez, the nurse and mom from Chelsea. The not so desperate New York housewife. 'Sophia Gemignani, did you not realize what you were doing? How close you came to ruining our lives?'

Tempest, that is what I said to her. Then, this Sophia, this Italian 30 something looks up at me dazed, as if slipping into a heroin looking induced dream state. She turns her lilac colored eyes upward, staring into my shaded brown ones, appalled as she recognizes me. Too shocked to even scream, I slip the blade into her chest, through the ironed white cotton blouse, into the side ventricles of the heart muscle I had studied so well in Anatomy 101. This is for you, Sophia, whose layered violet eyes think they are better than mine. Whose figure hasn't been stretched and stitched and sucked dry of its youth and tone. This is for taking Jerod from me. I move the knife around. I maneuver it. Christ! The blood! I withdraw it. The blood drips onto the ground. It spills all over my gloves. I pull them off of my hands and shove them and the dripping knife into the bag. For some reason I think of Thanksgiving and pulling turkey gizzards out from the insides; there is that damn word again: turkey. Tempest, help me."

Haven

And the dream ends.

I sit up perspiring and breathing short breaths. Who the hell is Haven? Why is she telling me all of this in my sleep? I take a deep breath, try to relax. Mario hasn't so much as stirred. He is at peace because he has never killed anyone like I have. He is at peace because he doesn't have the mission I now have. He is not a hurting woman. He is not a killer.

You may remember me. My name is Tempest Mc Tierney and I shared my life with you in a book called My Scorpio Soul. It became a best seller, by the way. So, I really do not have to worry very much about money right now. Phew.

My children are all adults now; I do worry about them. Then there is Mario. You must remember "Bedroom Eyes?" He was the Galveston detective with the two toned brown eyes that I was attracted to during the investigation of Creepo. Remember how he kept sneaking looks at me? I never wrote this before, because, after all, I was married and I am extremely loyal, but the truth is I thought about him a lot when I was in prison. And, finally, after several months of shy letters passing between us, he came to visit me.

But, he still wasn't Peter...

In case you never read my book: I ended up in prison for ten years for killing a stalker that terrorized my family and murdered my husband, Doctor Peter Mc Tierney. I wasn't, nor am I now a sociopath. I don't think so, anyway. That isn't to say there isn't a chance I could become one. No. That isn't to say there isn't a chance.

There is.

My children are now living in varied parts of the United States. My daughter, Sarah, is a documentary filmmaker. She is living in Los Angeles with her daughter, Molly, after a brief time trying out life in Boston. However, L.A. is more conducive to her vocation, so she moved West. Sadly, I missed the birth of my first grandchild. It is almost too painful for me to discuss this and the next few years of my children's lives that I was absent for. Sarah says if I can make it to California in early September, I can see Molly go to her first day of Kindergarten.

My sons, Kyle and Cody, the twins, still live in the northeast. Kyle teaches history at a small independent college and Cody is a music producer. They are thirty-two now and successful in all the ways a mother would want her children to be successful. They are happy. What warms my heart most is how kind they are to one another. The difficulties of having their father murdered and their mother incarcerated bonded them together in a way most siblings never experience. I don't tell them how prison changed me. I don't tell them about the dark tunnel I sometimes travel to.

When I got out of prison I had some real catching up to do. But, to be truthful, I haven't had a lot of time for that. Reading letters from desperate women who write to me on my website takes so much of my focus. That is where my story takes a turn. It has become less about me and more about my readers. My new passion in life has been to teach the women who write to me about saving their own souls. Yet, I can only pick one woman at time. It takes a lot of energy to save a soul.

I heard from Haven Rodriquez pretty quickly after my release. Yes. The one who spoke to me in my sleep; the one I dreamed about with the knife. Once I read her letter, I understood. I became connected to her and now I cannot get her out of my mind. I know I will have to save her. She is consumed with sadness. It is a combination of things. First, her husband's infidelity. Second, the guilt she feels for her part in it. Third, the extreme fear that he is gone forever. She fights the depression, but he hurt her. Her feelings exhaust me; that is how much I feel her pain. Mario has warned me to not get too involved with Haven any more than words of comfort. But, I know I will not be able to stifle my involvement with her. Inside my Scorpio soul, I yearn to help her. I feel the same desperation from her that I felt while Creepo abused us.

She wrote to me on my blog first. Did I tell you about the website that Sarah set up for me as soon as I was released? I posted my book tour schedule there, started a blog, and so on. Overnight I became a cult hero for women who feel like killing someone. Remember, in my case, I was left with no choice. However, these women have choices and I am trying my hardest to show them that.

Obviously, none of this was ever my intention, believe me. I had no idea women would write to me in such a desperate "Dear Abbey" fashion. Their letters have not been about their rebellious teens, sports obsessed husbands, or conflicts with in-laws. No, I am getting letters from women about death, murder, revenge, hurt, and betrayal. Earlier today, I had to go sit by the water and look for Dolphin Dad to discuss this with him. I worry that my past actions will cause others to put me on some ridiculous pedestal and someone may try to emulate me. Dolphin Dad, what do you say? Tell me what to do. Peter, can you hear me from heaven? Help me. Should I follow this new calling? I relate to these women's rage. I understand them. Is this insane? Or, am I absolutely sane? You see, my original intention sitting in that prison cell was to do my penance, wait for my release in humility, and let things be. But, when I got this following of fans, I got so drawn in. It didn't take too long before I was getting a thousand hits a week on my site, and almost as many letters.

Both my dream and Haven's initial letter froze me. I didn't reply. Then, after procrastinating and vacillating back and forth a million something times about how to reply; she called me. She was crying.

I was still deciding, you see, if I would go out on a limb for her or not. But it was her voice, with that trace of a Puerto Rican accent that truly jumped out and stayed there embedded in front of me. That made the decision for me. I felt such empathy for her. She was completely confused.

She confessed that her husband, Jerod, had suddenly disappeared. Yet, she wasn't sure if it was of his own free will or if it was foul play. She suspected he could have become involved in a second adulterous affair of their marriage of fifteen years. Or, he could have gone back to his "first" mistress (the one from my dream, Sophia). And, another possibility was that he could have been hurt, maybe even kidnapped or killed. This was a situation, she whispered almost inaudibly, that could be connected to where he worked.

She was in the dark. Or, so she claimed.

Haven is Aries. That means impulsive, creative, persistent, strong, a leader. On my blog I ask those writing to me to give a bit of information about themselves. Their zodiac sign is one of the first questions I ask. Usually, the person writing takes some time before they reveal their true "secrets." But Haven was different. From the very beginning she was gut wrenchingly honest. She admitted she had almost committed murder. Ahh. A woman after my own soul.

Did we share that dark place, I wondered? That place where you commit murder if it means protecting those you love? Of course we did. She would be joyous killing. Like I was. Do you ever think you are on the edge? I do. I am. I am told I should be consumed with guilt about killing Suong White, or "Creepo."

I have some shame; it is true. But consumed with guilt? Not a chance.

How could I have become so popular when I had committed murder, I wonder? Then I know. Like those rays of the sun's warmth that would touch my cheeks while lying on my cot in prison. Like the pastel colored clouds floating in the air around me. "God loves us and forgives us," my small, refined mother-in-

law told me. She whispered it to me when she and my father-in-law came all the way to the northeast from Texas one day to visit me. She leaned in, and under a new light blue beret, she whispered, "God loves you, Tempest. God forgives you." Then she winked.

She and my father-in-law remind me of Peter. They have parts of him in their eyes, their expressions, and their voices. When they visited, they told me all about my daughter Sarah and her apartment in a little suburb of Los Angeles called Sierra Madre, in the foothills above Pasadena. They filled me in about Cody's recording studio and his music business in Boston. How he had worked so hard to build up the right studio for the right clients. And, Kyle, how graceful and eloquent he is teaching and how his office in the small prestigious college where he now teaches is like a good, familiar bookstore; they said he is comfortable in his own skin.

I was so happy to hear about the kids; but it hurt. I was missing them so much. Have you ever heard the expression that something "hurts good"? It is sort of like when you get your teeth cleaned. It hurts, but it hurts in a good way? I had chosen not to see the kids while I was gone knowing it would be too hard. But hearing such vivid descriptions about them and their lives brought me back intimately to the tragedy I was living by not being able to share those years with them. When my in-laws left I went into such a depression. I cannot remember exactly when they came to visit, but I do remember asking them by letter not to come back. It was too hard.

"Why?" I asked Haven. "Why would this have happened to your husband? Where did he work? What did he do?" "He works for an investment firm being investigated for Ponzi fraud," she whispered.

Was Haven hiding the crimes of her husband? I sighed.

Does she want permission from me for something? Does she just assume I am some sort of sleuth because I had finally figured out who Creepo was when all the cops hadn't been able to prove anything? Creepo had stalked us for years, then followed us to another city, and, finally, committed murder. I had seen her on that hill behind our house in Portsmouth—standing up there watching; it was Suong White. That was all the proof I needed. Suong White had killed Peter as I suspected all along. Plus, I had Dolphin Dad to guide me; I wondered now, who does Haven have? There has to be an angel in your court or you simply cannot survive these things.

And, please do not laugh, but you know how I love the movies. Anyone I help has to love them, too. It doesn't matter what kind: old, classic, horror, thriller, romance, comedy, foreign. They have to be able to escape to the world of film or they would not be able to survive. Haven has to love the movies like I do. You see, we need that escape and we need it often. For instance, Haven mentioned the movie <u>The Lovely Bones</u> to me, based on a novel by Alice Siebold. I know why she mentioned this. It is because of the family. They are destroyed when Susie Salmon is murdered. The entire film is about this poor girl looking down on how her family falls apart before attempting to piece their lives back together after she is killed. I wonder: will that be Haven and her two sons if they discover Jerod is dead? Like how we were destroyed with Peter's murder? Except it is even worse with a child. There is something about hurting children. It is unforgivable. Children don't ask to be born, to be hit, to be hurt. To be murdered.

I get so depressed thinking about murder that I enter my dark tunnel again. I am the only one allowed inside.

Was my killing Creepo unforgivable? I decide it is forgivable based on her crimes. She was the criminal; I was the protector. Then, I resume thinking about Haven's dilemma. I do a little research on men who go missing. I find this on the Internet and I have paraphrased what I discovered: "They are not missing to themselves. It is only the people who are left behind who see them as missing. People who deliberately disappear are ready to do so; they do not see it as so bad. There is a small group of people who go missing for a week or two and then reappear not being able to remember what happened. For those who are missing for months or years, they could be suffering from some kind of dissociative amnesia or fugue, a condition caused by psychological stress. The US Medical Encyclopedia, the Merck Manual, describes dissociation fugue as: a disorder in which one or more episodes of sudden, unexpected, and purposeful travel from home (fugue) occur, during which a person cannot remember some or all of his past life. Most often found in those who have suffered in wars, accidents, or natural disasters, the condition typically lasts only hours or days, before the sufferer recovers all or part of his original identity. While "fugues" may be rare, it is clear that for most missing men, especially, the pressure on them has been immense. If the man (or woman) has had a complete breakdown and then he regains some sort of normal mental thinking, he will be horrified at what he has done and the effect it has had on those he loves." Hmmmm.

I have new information from Haven. By the way, do you remember that I had sent an arsenal of weapons north to Portsmouth to be stored and then I told everyone I had asked the kids to sell the guns?

I lied.

An intense vision abruptly fills and takes over my mind. I see "them" even though I have never even seen a photo. Jerod Rodriquez and Sophia Gemignani. I know already they are Haven's husband and his mistress. I shake my head to lose the vision but it possesses me. I am increasingly, more and more, a psychic in secret.

I have to watch:

Sophia gets him his favorite drink, a glass of white wine. She comes close to him and hands it to him not moving anything but her outreached hand. Is it already impossible for him? She bends toward him to hand him a napkin from the table and her breasts, partly revealed above a coral colored dress, brush against his face. Accidentally. Fat Chance. I feel the tension in him. I sense his excitement. He can hardly contain it. She has it, too. Without a word, she moves to the sofa and lies on her back across from him. She lets one leg fall to the side and drop off lazily. She exposes her beautiful pale leg, moisturized to perfection. He sips his wine and shifts in his seat. He stands, finishes the drink and goes to her. He is there, above her. His once tranquil green eyes are alive with fire. His guilt buried far beneath desire. She separates her legs and inches up her skirt. He doesn't need to search for a way in. He is already there.

What the hell? I am not an erotica visionary. Next, I see the color yellow and it looks like little wings flapping so fast, in fast motion. It is Haven's deceased aunt, Nana, in the after-life; she's come back to earth as a hummingbird. Her love for Haven overwhelms me. She spins around me as she tells me I must help Haven.

ABOUT JEROD AND ME

Chapter 1

By: Haven

Dear Tempest:

I have always, always wished my name were Heaven instead of Haven. Mainly, I have wanted this because as a kid my dad used to whistle and sing that song, "Cheek to Cheek," that Frank Sinatra sang and Fred Astaire danced to. Basically, the story goes like this: my name was supposed to be Heaven, but the volunteer at the hospital made a mistake and wrote "Haven" on the birth certificate. Now, I just want to be where I was always meant to be. In heaven, I mean. Here's the song my dad sang when I was growing up: "Cheek to Cheek."

"Heaven, I'm in heaven And my heart beats so that I can hardly speak And I seem to find The happiness I seek when we're out together dancing cheek to cheek."

I have never felt so far away from heaven as I do right now. I am worried. I feel like I do not know myself anymore. I am trying so hard to figure out what I want. I want to preserve my soul. I have to. The question is: do I save myself alone or as a part of my family? I have lost myself somewhere in the air between holding onto my family and holding onto myself. I could lose both. Or, I could keep both. And Jerod. I may have already lost him.

Tempest, you have asked me to write down the facts. I am Aries. I like art and I love to cook. I am a nurse. I have two sons ages 10 and 13. I had my children very late in life. I am impulsive and bold. My boldness has grown even stronger of late and comes from another part of me. It finds its way climbing out of every branch of me to keep my family safe. My husband committed adultery and admitted it to me. I do not want to be divorced. I do not want to be single. I want the connection of love with my husband. He is a good person. I want to share my grandchildren with the man I chose to marry nearly 15 years ago.

I am not perfect. He is not perfect.

I am about to go to jail because I stabbed my neighbor who I do not trust and it is all because of Jerod. He is missing. Let me explain. Please, be patient with my story. This is all so new to me. His being gone. His cheating last year. Cops not trusting me. Our life now fractured.

Jerod Rodriquez is a handsome man. All 6 feet 2 inches of him. Half Caucasian and half Puerto Rican, he stood out in his college class for the perfect English that he spoke even though his genes make him look more ethnic than White. When we first met, the brown, thick, generous head of hair that waved in dark swirls with brief sun touched highlights around his temples seemed perfectly placed beside his coffee colored complexion. People were always surprised about his English. But they couldn't know, of course, how hard he had worked for that inflection in his speaking. He sought to appear and sound a certain way. He believed it would help in his success in the business world, and he was right. It did. He impressed the hell out of people after he graduated from Cornell with an MBA.

Yet today, in his early 50's, Jerod couldn't look any more different from the man he was in 1980. Oh, it isn't only age that has changed him really. For the most part, he has maintained his good looks. However, in recent months he had withered down to 150 pounds. He looks battered, like the strength he once had seeped away along with his will to live. I have no idea how psychosomatic it is, but since his disappearance, now I am losing weight, too. Could it be we are so connected that I am feeling his pain?

Ay dios mio!

Haven

I AM IN JAIL AND I'M DREAMING

Chapter 2

By: Haven

Dear Tempest:

MY DREAM:

It is night. Jerod and I are dancing in the middle of my jail cell. Moonlight pours through the windows and shines off the floor bouncing shadows across our faces. I run my fingers down Jerod's back. The moment is sweet and erotic. He slowly draws his fingers down over my face, gently caressing my forehead, my eyes, and my lips. He slides his hands under my prison T-shirt, slowly moving them up toward my breasts. My breathing slows. We dance silently, my hair swaying under a low hanging tropical ceiling fan that doesn't even really exist. Sensuously, Jerod presses into me. I am biting my lip. He is looking right into my eyes as he strokes my chest, I slowly begin moving my fingers down his torso, around the curve of his hips, and then I am digging into the back of his jeans. Suddenly, I hear footsteps. Sophia appears at the door. She reaches out her hand to him and he steps back from me. They embrace tenderly.

    I wake up crying. I feel so guilty for losing my cool with Canan (I will explain all about this in the next entry), our Turkish neighbor I don't trust; and now, because of that, the boys are home with my dear friend Amber and here I sit in my jail cell awake from this dream and waiting for my attorney to get me out of here. But, my real freedom is questionable. That is because what I need is freedom of the heart, freedom of the mind, and freedom of my soul. I in a different "sort of" prison. The prison of my imagination. I have decided since they have offered it, I will talk to the jail therapist. This happened because of everything: my dream, "them", the stabbing, missing the boys, missing Jerod.

She told me I am strong after I spilled my guts to her. Don't they say that to everyone? "You're so strong." What the hell does that mean? I don't feel strong. She got me to talk about it all. She had me make association lists about us. It felt good to unload. Then she told me to picture my life alone, without Jerod. She had me make a list of goods and bads in our marriage, pros and cons.

That was last night and I slept worse than ever. It might be from talking it all out loud. It made everything even worse because I couldn't pretend anything anymore. I couldn't pretend that my marriage was what I used to think it was.

I am the one who is lonely now.

Maybe therapists are like chiropractors: the pain gets worse before it gets better. Or, perhaps I had been living in my little bubble dream world for so long before Sophia came along, that the pain and pretense was always there just waiting to erupt like a sudden tsunami that I had refused to evacuate. I didn't heed the warnings. I have read that marriages can be better after being on such shaky ground. I now stand on the periphery of my life staring in and unsure. I stood on the outside contemplating. And hurting.

As a nurse we learn panic plays no part in our profession. I have tried to adapt that to the rest of my life as well. I don't panic. But, that doesn't mean I do not feel deeply.

I will start from the beginning.

A year ago Jerod had an extramarital relationship with a woman named Sophia Gemignani. He told me about it after breaking it off with her. It lasted two months. Right after he told me about it, a horrible combination of emotions kept consuming me. My warmth belied the cold inside of me. I was now freezing. Jerod's confession to me was like a tear in my heart. Like he poked a hole and let the cold air in. But, that isn't the only reason for my letter, Tempest. You see, he is gone. He just disappeared. He never came home one day and I am not sure why. That is the other reason for my letter,

I am not sure if he left, or, was taken from us.

The cops have talked to everyone including work associates, neighbors, family, the boys' teachers, shop owners that know us, her family, her apartment manager, etc. Meanwhile, this hell catches our family inside its fire.

La puta.

Haven

THE REASON I AM IN JAIL

Chapter 3

DAY #5 of Jerod being gone

By: Haven

Dear Tempest:

I stabbed Canan and I got myself arrested. It was just three days ago now that I grabbed the knife on my way leaving the apartment. I already knew what I would do.

    Jerod had been gone for two days, and the cops were skeptical that it was foul play by his employers; instead, they looked suspicious of me when I told them about the adultery. I realized at that point how hard it is to get attention for missing persons before they are truly missing for at least three or four days, especially somewhere like Manhattan. So many people are reported missing who aren't and that is why it isn't taken so seriously for the first two days. But, back to the knife. I had stuck it into my purse, walked down the hall and knocked on Canan's door. It is this little jagged knife we always use at my house to slice bagels. That day, I admit, I was a little nuts. When she opened the door, I peeked over her shoulder. There was a single coral colored tulip in a vase just like the ones Jerod used to bring home to me. On the floor stood some luggage. I panicked he might be hiding in her apartment, to leave with her. I was so paranoid now. Deep down, I wonder even now, did he wish he had just left for good the first time?

Tempest, sometimes now when I see older (mature) women, I see me. I see me in their faces. Their eyes hold the secrets of men who yelled at them or men who cheated on them. Their eyes show the angst of their children's bad decisions, the loss of their best friends or siblings with sickness, age, or conflicts. But, the most hurt is in the eyes that have had regrets, have had to learn to forgive, have tried to forget, have kept private thoughts private with no friends' eyes or ears to share them with. I see me now in the eyes of other women who have tried to forget.

We are a secret club.

On that day Canan acted arrogant with me when I inquired about Jerod, I was so sure she was lying that I reached inside my purse, pulled that jagged edge knife out and plunged it into her shoulder. Not her neck, not her eye, her shoulder. (Remember, I am a nurse. So I did know what I was doing in a sick, academic sort of way). She screamed and screamed as if she had rehearsed it for months. Like in <u>Psycho.</u> You knew I would say that, didn't you? You knew that because you realize how much you and I have in common. Instead of helping her, I collapsed in a heap on the cold tile floor beside her. As I fell, I remembered your stalker Creepo falling when she died... and Peter falling when Creepo struck him. We all fall down. When the kids were small, Jerod and I would play <u>Duck, Duck Goose</u> outside on the roof deck with them. Then, <u>Ring around the Rosie</u>; yes, "we all fall down."

We are all falling now.

Blood gushed out of Canan's shoulder and a neighbor applied pressure to stop it. Canan was now slumped against the wall and I was lying on the floor beside her. I pretended I had fainted. People ran out of their apartments and started screaming at the frenetic commotion. Then, I did faint. Christ. What had I done?

Then, I was arrested.

As a result of my stabbing, the kids are now without a mom at home either. But, I won't be in here for long. Canan is not pressing charges. Of course, only I know there is some reason and it has to be because she is involved with Jerod's disappearance. She wants to stay out of this limelight; she wants to stay out of the picture. The cops are baffled. Jeremy, my older son who is our "old soul," told me on the phone he had the feeling that the police seemed enamored with Canan and convinced that I had done something to Jerod. He is young to be so perceptive. They've now interviewed the Tariks, Jerod's employers; perhaps they came away with some suspicions about the company, but if they did, they shared nothing with me. That all strikes me as incredibly odd. And the suit cases on the floor in Canan's apartment I saw. Where was she going?

Haven

MARIO BRINGS ME DAISIES

Chapter 4

By: Tempest

Mario began to bring me daisies, which is just right since I savored two colored roses in my heart for only Peter. Daisies marked a new start. A second chance that I never thought I would get. And Mario knew I was innocent in the sense that only pure loyalty for my husband and family would drive me to kill. Mario helped save me; he really did.

At the same time, incarceration was living hell and I paid my dues. You may not agree. After all I had murdered. But, I murdered a murderer. I tell myself I am a female Robin Hood. I rid the world of a freakish nightmare. Then, I stuck to my dictum and never allowed my kids to visit me while I was incarcerated. They needed to get on with their own lives. I didn't want their weekends preoccupied with coming upstate to see their mother. Oh sure, at first they bucked up against it. And, we exchanged many letters. I missed them terribly. This was the worst part of my penance. I could barely deal with not seeing my children.

Mario understood and helped so much. He would bring stories to read to me. He brought *games we could play like Scrabble. He knew I needed not only romance, but distractions as well. Funny, isn't it? And then, because he was so accustomed to the prison system, he bought DVDs for the library so we would get to actually watch relatively new films. When I was in there, I also saw some of my favorite classic films, thanks to Mario. Like <u>The Birds</u> by Hitchcock, and <u>The Godfather</u> by Coppola. Towards the tail end is when I watched the first two seasons of a TV series called <u>Dexter</u>. I have to admit it frightened me how much I could relate to Dexter.*

On the day I was released, I was almost resentful that Mario was there at the gate with my kids, he and the older Vietnamese man were standing beside Sarah, Kyle and Cody. I had told Mario that I wanted to see the children alone. But he came anyway. Later, he claimed it was to protect me. He wanted to make sure I was okay, that the kids were okay. That was pretty intuitive of Mario. After all, he had no way of knowing that Suong White's father would show up at my release.

Also, during the last months before my release, without having told me, Mario moved to New Hampshire. He knew long before I did that I would fall in love with him. His mother, a gentle soul, knew this as well. She even gave him her engagement ring from her first marriage to a WWII veteran for when he proposed. She knew that if her son was finally ready to settle down, at forty-four, then it had to be the right gal. Mothers know their sons. Poor thing. Somehow, someday he would have to explain to her he was marrying a killer. Sometimes I cannot believe how Mario waited so long for me to get out of prison. We get the strangest rewards in life.

Then, the day I was released, there he was. Beside Suong's father, beside my children and my grandchild. Bittersweet, you see, because the kids had no idea I loved him. They didn't know we had gotten so close. Furthermore, every so often, Mario has no idea how, when I look at him, at times I am wishing I am looking at Peter. That is one of my Aries secrets.

But, back to Haven. Helping her to do anything illegal is out of the question. I vow I will never risk my freedom again. My incarceration was just too hard, not only on me. It was very hard on the kids. I have only been on the "outside" for a few months. I only just bought a yoga mat in a pretty violet color. I just dug my old photo albums out to look over because I had missed poring over them so much while I was "away." I still need peaceful time. I want time to visit the kids at their jobs, go for walks with old friends, go see Peter's parents who are still alive and golfing in south Florida. Plus, as soon as I got out and started this blog, I had told my story. Then my simple life was left waiting while these pleas for help came from women all wanting advice. I couldn't believe my new vocation of advising hurt and desperate women. I began to answer them. All the while, I couldn't stop thinking about Haven.

First of all, her name being almost "Heaven," but not quite. Where was that damn first "e?" Was it a typo or was her name truly one letter away from heaven? Then her sign: impulsive, impetuous, creative, strong, a leader. Yet, she sounded so meek, so vulnerable. And there you have it, why I need to see Dolphin Dad. I look further into the water and there he was, my father, leaping. "Yes! Help her!" He is yelling in his leaping sort of way off the coast of Portsmouth, my new home. I can hear the high school's marching band practicing in the distance. Tonight, under the crescent shaped moon, I can hear the sounds of a saxophone lace the air that is thick with Haven's story and her plight. And I know that the dark cloud that once ruined my life was now ruining Haven's.

SCARY THINGS HAVE HAPPENED TO ME

Chapter 5

By: Haven

Dear Tempest:

I was chased on foot a few days before Jerod went missing. I had brought in Jerod's old mandolin to a musical instrument repair shop on Greenwich Avenue in the West Village. Ishmael is the owner's name. I was involved in a conversation with him when a tall man wearing a black hooded sweatshirt stared through the window into the store. I must have gasped. His face was too darkly shadowed by his hood for me to see who he was. Ishmael looked up. "He's just looking at the window display, Haven. What's the matter with you?" (Ishmael and I go way back) "I'm not sure. Maybe I've seen him before," I lied. Of course I was already suspecting it was Aihyan from Tariks' Inc., Jerod's investment firm. Ishmael shrugged, "It's a big city. Takes all kinds. Let's get back to your mandolin. It's around fifteen years old. It is in beautiful shape. You say it's Jerod's?" I nodded. "I am thinking about getting new strings, getting it all cleaned up for him. A tune up." He nodded. But I couldn't get the tall man with the hood that could be Aihyan out of my mind. Ishmael and I decided on what was needed for the mandolin. I left the store. I was a little scared, but determined to see this man up close.

I decided to walk. It was only around twenty blocks to my house, not so far by NY standards. It was a bustling time of day: lunch hour. I walked straight toward Chelsea. Then, I turned around and there he was again. I knew it. I began to walk faster. He did, too. When I got to Highline Park, the new park that runs through Chelsea along an old rail line, I turned around and he was gone. I sat down on one of the chaises and leaned back, trying to piece the nightmare that is my life now back together.

That was also the day that the apartment felt different. Violated. Someone had been inside. While I had my head back resting, someone went inside our home and walked around. When I got home I heard something, it was as quick as a harsh breeze, a dash of uneasiness. He was just leaving! There was yellow spinning outside the kitchen window. Nana, my ghostly hummingbird protector, was flummoxed. She had watched him come and go and couldn't do a thing about it.

I walked around slowly. Pillows were in their places. The kitchen still needed some dishes to be washed, sweeping of the tiles called out to me, garbage pleaded to be carried downstairs. Blinds were up and blinds were down, all in the right places. Then I saw. The chair. The cushions were not sitting in their correct positions. It is an odd chair with too many cushions. Jerod and I had liked it when we first spotted it at the outdoor flea market in Hell's Kitchen, despite its being a bit unusual. It is a pretty earth tone of rust colors, with leaves and blossoms. But the bottom cushion was jutting out. I knew because there is a method to the madness of adjusting this chair and its odd combination of pillows and it took some learning on our part. "Jerod?" I called. Of course he wasn't home. At that point, he was still at work.

Someone had been inside our apartment and they had messed with my odd pillow chair. Why? Who? My life was already spiraling, even before Jerod's disappearance. I had no idea all that would transpire soon after that day and how long it would be until I could finally write to you.

I felt lost. I cracked my knuckles, stretched my neck around like a cat trying to decide what I needed to do next. I had taken a visual imagery class at the local adult education center. It was supposed to be for visualizing positive changes in our lives. Could I call on that now? For example, I was told to enclose myself with white, or picture a home I would like to eventually own. Or, I was encouraged to see myself thinner, or happier in some way. At least that's what the teacher thought I was working on. I had signed up before Jerod went missing. I told her that I had been struggling with my self-image ever since Jerod told me about him and Sophia. And let's be honest. I had always struggled with it, but it was worse now. Funny how I felt more comfortable telling perfect strangers about something so personal than those I know. She told me there is a reason for negative things in our lives. We sometimes have to have these things happen to make room for change--*God closes a door but opens a window sort of thing.* But as she spoke to me, all I could think of was how no one except for my friend, Amber, would ever know the truth about Jerod, me and Sophia.

Instead of visualizing positive things I go negative in a ballistic way. I close my eyes and as I do every day; I picture Sophia and Jerod; then I practice visual imagery of me slapping her, hard; next I am placing a pointy rusted nail into her car tires. I'm doing mean things that probably would never hurt her one bit as much as she has hurt me. But, it helps. So, I smile. Then, my favorite image: I am on a ferry; it is somewhere gorgeous like the Pacific Northwest off the Washington coast. I remember how Michael Douglas took a ferry in the movie, <u>Disclosure,</u> when he is accused by Demi Moore of sexual harassment. Sophia is standing at the same railing, dark hair blowing in the breeze with the deep blue, cold Northwest waters stretched out in front of her. I see her so clearly in my mind's eye. I wondered then, did she understand the power in her beauty was in the contrast? The purple eyes and dark hair so in contrast to the pale face and red lips. My instincts are sharp and it takes control of me so that it feels eerily real. I am stronger than I allow myself to act. I am far away and I can't see her closely, yet, I know intimately how she feels. Somehow, the railing snaps and she stumbles and falls into the frigid water splashing quietly. No one notices but me. She waves her arms for help. *The arms that encircled my husband.* I am standing closer now, bundled in a big, thick purple jacket that matches those eyes. *I do not move.* Our eyes lock. She knows the truth. *I will not save her.* I look over at an orange life preserver jacket and a white tube that I can throw to her. *If I want.* But I don't. I look around. No one has noticed. The boat is getting farther away from her now. A shark's fin pops up. Then another appears. They are circling her. Her hair, wet, and her face with those Liz Taylor eyes, bob up and down until she disappears, terror drowning in the waves. Her head bobs back up for an instant. I find my voice.

I scream, "Woman overboard!" The water around her turns dark red first, then it fixes into a deep purple, a mixture of blood and blue rushing in swirls around her. Sooner or later everyone has to pay his or her due. A man runs over to the broken railing and peers out as he grabs a megaphone on the hook beside the preserver. He yells into the megaphone, glances at me incredulous, and then runs toward the captain's quarters.

I feign shock and sadness, and the water is a soft lavender now. Like your own ghost's color, Dolphin Dad's aura. Then, it is blue again. ***I smile***.

Haven

DEAR TEMPEST

Chapter 6

DAY #6 of Jerod being gone.

By: Haven

Dear Tempest:

At least you succeeded in getting rid of your hell. You killed the monster that murdered Peter. What do I get to do? I only get to do visual imagery of what I want to happen to her. These sick, selfish, narcissistic women who think they are right and we are wrong. Meanwhile, I sit and wait at the disposal of others and their decisions. I am still in the dark. I imagine Jerod's death. I think the most frustrating thing about this whole situation has been the energy I have given away to mere survival. Also, the amount of space this terror has taken up inside my head, between my ears and in the gray matter that used to be a very good brain. The stuff I do not know. The stuff I do know: he has been missing for 6 days now. The police are following some leads, but nothing so far...

My story is stranger than fiction. It is strangely familiar and unfamiliar at the same time. I have only just entered hell. Oh, now that is a lie. I was in hell last year, too. The most painful hell. My life was a twisted mess then, too.

Hell.

I have always believed in doing the right thing. Do you remember Ashley Judd in <u>Double Jeopardy</u>? Ashley decided to kill her horrific husband that she had been accused of murdering, but in reality, he had never even died. He had tricked her, taken their son, and moved in with the boy's pre-school teacher. Then, he changed his identity and moved to New Orleans. The rat bastard! I just love movies about New Orleans. You can almost feel the river's balmy breeze, smell the gumbo, taste the food in the French Quarter.

I remember when you and Peter ate po' boys on your ride out of Galveston. Ever since then I have been craving one. But when you got home those flowers were all over your lawn. Those damn flowers Creepo had cut down and left for you.

Back to <u>Double Jeopardy</u>. When Ashley finally found her husband alive and well in the Quarter, she had learned about double indemnity: you can't be indicted twice of murdering the same person. She is my other hero. I really don't care about rumors that she is difficult to work with on movie sets. She is gorgeous. I love every single movie she and Morgan Freeman are in together; those movies that are based on books written by James Patterson. And here I am, pretending I am Ashley Judd, beautiful and spunky and a good friend to Morgan. Ashley, who went to prison for a long time (in this movie) like you, away from her family. You pretended to be Demi;

I am Ashley.

There is a gorgeous rainbow is as if it is just waiting for me to run and jump up and be lifted to the pot of gold waiting on the other side:

The other side of these walls.

My best friend in the whole world, Amber, is here right now with my boys. One is in his young teens and has a girlfriend, sort of. My other son, Justin, is still a little boy. Yes, you are right. We had kids very late. I was forty-four when I had Justin and forty-one when I had Jeremy. Justin is ten. But it will go so fast, and then he will shoot up inches, and he will have a girlfriend, too.

Yo tengo mucho amor para Jerod. Ay dios mio.

I need to resume my correspondence later. I can hear the sound of the guard's handcuffs coming down the hall. The custodian waxed the floors last night, so her shoes are squeaking. Like fingernails on a chalkboard. And she is thin, so there is no swishing of her thighs together, just the clanking of cuffs. Now I can hear the keys. I look out the high window at my rainbow one last time. Is it really finally there for me? Then I remember She is still out there somewhere. Sophia.

She twisted us all up.

La puta! Ugly, selfish, gorgeous, hourglass-perfect Sophia. But he had extricated himself from her and came back to us. I am reminded of that one line in <u>Unfaithful</u>, the movie starring Richard Gere and

Diane Lane, when her friend tells her, "they always end disastrously," about affairs.

You see, I love him. Ay dios mio!

But then this mess, and I wonder all over again; did Jerod have yet another affair? A second affair with this lady from Istanbul? This woman who had come to New York to go to graduate school, or so she lied. When I checked records of her attendance, as far back as I could, there was no sign of her. Who the hell was she? It was like she just appeared in the apartment next door with her thin, athletic figure and her henna dipped short hair. Her big green eyes accented with dark eyeliner, and her rear end, firm like a teenager's. How unfair is that? A perfect fanny right next door. Canan and her perfect derriere that probably has some little lady bug tattoo on it. Otra puta!

The thin guard is standing here fiddling with the keys in the lock and my boys are waiting outside, so loyal. They have brown eyes bright with stars of hopes and dreams.

Because they are young.

The prison therapist had a field day with me, telling me "we" have a lot of issues we will need to deal with if he comes home alive. That I cannot let the two of us just continue on without help, without counsel. Perhaps she is right. I accidentally said out loud that I know women loved him. Did I actually say, "loved?" like he is already dead? Jerod, are you alive?

You owe me to be alive.

The guard finally opens the cell door and steps aside, smiling widely. She is happy. In the few days I have been here we have become fast friends. She knows I am not like the others. She understands I did what I did (the stabbing) to protect my family, not because I am a demented, violent, psychopathic criminal. I nod at her, my Aries soul pounding with heartache.

I look down at this, my letter to you. I stand with my yellow pad and carry it as if I am a proud waitress carrying a t-bone steak, garlic mashed potatoes and broccoli. Dios, yo tengo hambre! Then, before I move from this place forever, I see her. Nana, my mother's sister. She is always there, in her ethereal cloud. Just like your father. She is spinning her wings in joy, just ahead of the slim guard, but then, she surprises me. Magically she is outside my window when I glance back for a final time; she is there, the yellow-clouded hummingbird that never leaves me. I think Nana became a hummingbird because when alive she loved to hum. She loved gardens, and colored glass. Hummingbirds come right up to those feeders made of pretty colored glass to eat there. I close my eyes and listen to Nana humming and am reminded of beach glass. I can never find any when I look for it. Maybe one day I will... Meanwhile, Nana must be causing quite a stir outside.

We stop to get my few belongings and I sign for them. I hear the abrasive buzzer and the guard leads me out to the outer gate. Justin has his mouth open ready to talk, like always. Jeremy is stepped back, but the protectiveness spills out of his eyes. The gate squeaks wider and I step out into the once misty day that now has a sun high in the sky with that rainbow over our heads. A moan is closer to what the hum of a hummingbird sounds like: a sad moan. But, Nana's is so graceful because she knows I am going home.

All at once, my sons rush at me and hold me tight, squeezing for space. And my mind thinks of something random: does my humming nana know your swimming dolphin dad?

Haven

NOW WHAT?

Chapter 7

By: Tempest

Sigh. She has left me hanging now, this Haven woman who stabbed her neighbor who could or could not be mistress #2, and loves her husband but isn't sure if he is being unfaithful or if he has been killed. The nurse, the mom, the Aries artist. Am I the chosen one to help Haven find heaven? I'm in, pulled way in. This woman who keeps going back and forth between love and hate, rage and adoration. She just got out of jail, having been there for only 3 days.

I pick up my cell phone to send Sarah a text. "Get your vaccinations before you go." I type this painstakingly. I may be hip enough to text, but it isn't without pain. Suddenly, my phone beeps that I have a reply. I assume it is from Sarah. It isn't. It's from Haven. It reads: "Maybe Canan killed him."

I write to her and ask her to share more. I need a lot more insight into this woman. If I help her we need to be discreet. I never want to go back to prison but this overwhelming urge to kill again comes over me. Like an itch I want to scratch. Damn it. I want to help her and if it means I need to murder again, then so be it. Did I actually just say that? I can't *do that again! I can only offer advice. She told me she has kept a journal. She needs to share it with me. I need to see what happened not only recently, but a year ago with the two of them. What sort of man is Jerod? Where did he go? How did it happen? Perhaps, by getting to know more about their history together, I can piece some ideas about "now" together. Haven doesn't seem sure about anything. She is still raw with hurt, but she is also strong. An Aries through and through.*

My hope is if I read her journals as the times played out in real life, back from a year ago, I will be able to see into them, and see the truth; maybe even more than in her recounting of it all now. I can come to my own conclusions about Jerod. Oh, dear reader, do you think I should be getting involved with someone like Haven? Maybe I should only be listening and refusing to advise her at all. I do want to help her. I cannot even imagine the pain of my spouse cheating on me and then disappearing. I think about Harrison Ford and Kristen Scott Thomas and how they discovered their spouses had been sleeping with each other before they died. This is the premise in a movie called <u>Random Hearts</u>. They had to deal with that betrayal as well as grieve their spouses' deaths. Complicated stuff!

And... she is a nurse. That is so interesting. Do you recall that atrocious story about the psychopathic nurse in England who was killing little children in the pediatric ward of the hospital where she worked? Of course, I killed, but I am no sociopath or psychopath. Creepo was both of those things, and sadistic. I am a woman who was left with no choice. Do you really think I was going to drive around my little coastal town of Portsmouth looking for her (Creepo) for the rest of my life? Do you suppose I could ever have gone for a walk again without constantly looking over my shoulder? No. Creepo had to be stopped. The trick was after that to remain sane in prison. I did a lot of reading. I did a lot of yoga. I did a lot of meditating. It feels as if I have lost some of that peace. That is just so strange. Inside prison all I did was dream of getting out. Now that I am out, I crave the peace of no interruptions. I crave the protection the guards offer. But not in the cell. Maybe I need to stay out of Haven's hell, out of her Aries secrets. It is just not fair to my family, or to Mario. Then, I look again at my "inbox" and it tells me I have new mail. Here goes...

JOURNAL ENTRIES FROM LAST YEAR

Chapter 8

By: Haven

Dear Tempest:

Well, these are what you asked for. I wrote all of them during the worst 2 months of our marriage. I scanned them to you from a copy scanner near Central Park. Then I sat in the sun at Columbus Circle and watched people enjoy the day wondering who else was depressed. How morbid I am.

2008- Christmas Eve

Feliz Navidad. Que pasa? What a horrible Christmas so far. Jerod has been mute. He sits on the couch and stares at the Maple tree outside our window void of leaves. He used to notice when the feather light leaves turned to a robust red and orange, but lately he hasn't noticed things like the leaves' colors. Something has possessed him. Where has he gone? Is it depression? Or is it even worse? He still comes back or rises to the occasion if one of the boys asks him to play ball, or watch a movie. I went and got the Christmas tree with Justin; Jerod has almost no interest whatsoever. What is he thinking about? Is it another woman? I look at him and he looks away. Is he hiding something? I am sick to my stomach. I shrink inside my robe and melt down into the floors. Like the wicked witch in The Wizard of Oz.

This is already the worst Christmas of my life. I can tell. The white blinking lights on our little Christmas tree go bright and then black, white with all the beautiful colors of the ornaments beside them, and then dark, just like Jerod. He keeps going into some sort of darkness I cannot reach. I wish now I had put some other colored lights on the tree that just remained constant. I should have done that. Maybe then he would remain constant.

2009- January 1

It is New Year's Day. Last night he left and took a walk through Central Park without me. *Jerod, how could you have done that? You know I love the park, any time of year.* At least that is where you claim you went. In the midst of hundreds of thousands of people screaming to welcome the New Year, you left alone. Your brown wool sweater smelled like Scotch when you returned. Covered in beautiful fresh snowflakes and smelling of Scotch. Are you drinking now? Since when? You weren't here with me to see Dick Clark and how he struggles to speak now after his stroke when the ball came down. We always watch Dick Clark. This cannot be. I was here alone, the TV remote in my hand, just waiting for you. I kept rewinding your favorite movie for you so that when you came in the door you would sit beside me and watch it and relax. That is how much I love you. I want you to relax. Instead, you came in with snow sprinkled on your broad shoulders, flakes on your moustache, shaky, reeking of stale liquor and not yourself. Is the not yourself part from suddenly drinking too much? I shut my eyes and pretended I was asleep. What secret are you harboring in those hazel eyes of yours? Or, maybe it is debt, or, God forbid, a health issue? Jesus, how I hope it is just money or cancer or a bad heart we are facing. I am so worried; our world is collapsing around us and I hlave no inkling why. You nicked yourself shaving in two spots. That is so unlike you. In a retributive sense, if you are sleeping with someone else, then, damn it, you deserve it and it makes sense, now doesn't it? When you play with fire, you get burned. And so do I just because I am your wife. That is how marriage works. If you hurt, I hurt. If you get burned, I get burned and maybe even more. Just like Tempest when her eye bled out. Because of Creepo, her eye bled and she had to go see that sweet, handsome Doctor Falsett. Tempest didn't deserve to suffer, but it made sense. Her eye bled trying so hard to see who Creepo was. You are nicking yourself because of what you are doing. What are you doing? On one hand, I feel sympathy. Of course I do. I have loved you for a long time. *You are my best friend.*

    I almost veer my car into a bus along the side of the street. I think, "Why not? You have ruined my life." I head toward the Hudson. Maybe I should drive into the cold, heartless river and let a touring bus roll over me and suffocate any life I have left inside of me. Is that what you want of me? I will remember this month as the worst month of my life.

2009- January 15th

It is Martin Luther King Day. You couldn't find your keys this morning and we found them in the refrigerator. Hiding behind a lemon yogurt.

Today is supposed to be about peace but it isn't. You just snapped at me for almost no reason.

Are you sleeping with someone else? But how can that be when you brought me my favorite flowers yesterday? I refuse to ask you any questions. It is fatalistic at this point. Plus, in a way it is lowering myself to ask you that question that feels too much like a bad Lifetime movie. Too cliché. "Are you having an affair?" I will never utter those words. If you are, you will have to tell me. We are not a cliché couple, Jerod. You will have to tell me if that is what is going on. Most women would say confront you.

I need to believe that you will tell me whatever it is you want to tell me when you are ready.

I will pray. A lot.

Last night while I lay there wondering what is going on, I rubbed Johnson's baby lotion into my feet. The pink lotion that has never changed. It has had the same consistency, the same smell, the same good vibes since I used it on the boys when they were babies. Tonight my feet smelled like that as I remember how I would massage the boys with lotion after their baths. I like to rub my toes together under the sheets after I put the lotion on. They slide toward each other in secret, slippery harmony under the white coolness of

Egyptian cotton. Funny the things that make us feel at peace. But you are my husband—shouldn't I feel some peace with you? Isn't that part of love? Feeling safe and feeling peace? Right now, I feel none. You have left me not only physically, but also emotionally. Someone else possesses you now. I can feel it. It breaks my heart. Is it love for her or fear I will find out that keeps you so distant?

Plus, I have run out of my favorite perfume you usually replace for me. And, even though I have left it there on the bathroom sink, empty, for you to see, you haven't noticed. A year ago you went to get me some as soon as I ran out. Did it stop smelling so subtle and beautiful on me? Or, did you just stop caring how I smell?

It's the perfume. The perfume you didn't get for me this year. The perfume you didn't notice was all gone.

I know the truth now.

2009- February 1

It has been two weeks since I have known the truth and haven't wanted to face it. I keep trying to convince myself I am wrong. Then, I think, it is really actually possible that you are in love with someone else. It is early in the morning and I have just woken up; I look at your spot beside me again. You are gone. Where? It is so damn early. Did we need more coffee? I hear the key and you are back. You always come back.

But will that always be so? What's the matter and why can't you talk to me? Life isn't supposed to be so horrible.

But, still I am silent. My favorite perfume, still empty. I refuse to let go. I refuse to stop loving you. I refuse to let you be this man you have stooped to. You are better than this. So be that man. Where did the man go that I fell in love with?

2009-February 3

The bank called to talk about a debt and some options we have. I wasn't really sure what they were talking about and then they said $32,000 dollars. It has to be a mistake. I told them so. But tonight, when you got home and I mentioned this, it was like your face caved in on itself. Your eyes turned gray and murky, and so did the color of your skin. I thought you were going to have a heart attack like your Uncle Darryl; do you remember how gray his face looked when we visited him in the hospital the night after he had a heart attack, the night before he died? You had that same color in your face.

Oh God, give me strength. What have you done? Why is this happening? I am beginning to understand divorce. People say it is the worst experience to go through, but could it be any worse than this? I doubt it. Is this why they say, "Murder, yes. Divorce, never."?

2009- February 6

It is Jeremy's 13th birthday and you forgot. That isn't like you. And you still haven't effectively explained to me why that debt has accrued and is so large. Some lame explanation about refinancing credit cards and an equity line. You must think I am stupid. God, how I wish I had been more of top of expenses. Now I have no way of ever knowing the truth because you do all the money stuff. Cop out that I am, I should have been more in tune with this. I was so lazy. But at least I am smart in one way. I know you are so tortured that no amount of debt, and no amount of money issues equals the pain you have in your eyes. Like Tempest knew when Peter was giving up, I know you are guilty.

You are hiding this deep and dark secret. It is killing you at the same time. I try to give you the confidence in me that you can tell me; but, instead, you are stoic and quiet. You and your secret.

Many of the painful situations we encounter in life are likely to be because we have failed to live according to our hearts, talents and natural plan.

I read this somewhere and the older I get, the more I agree. I think we have different family backgrounds, different heartbeats. We have different talents that we need to follow, no matter what age. We are so much who we grew up with. We are our parents. We are the houses we slept in, the vacations we took, the clothes we wore. We are the pets we had, the seasons we smelled, the colors of the trees. Those are the reasons so many marriages do not work. We have such different expectations of ourselves and others. Did I push you away?

Jerod, today I looked outside on the street when the blizzard stopped. The sky is dark, dark gray. I saw a man hidden under a hat staring up at our apartment building. He was tall, angular looking, a bit like Aihyan. Was it him? Why was he staring up at our place?

2009- February 10th

Today, Jeremy had a sax lesson. He forgot the music at home and he had to rush back to get it. He is talented. I love listening to him play. Jerod, you used to play the clarinet, but that has long since stopped. But, lately, I can tell you are tempted to take it up again. And the mandolin. I loved hearing you strum it. Sometimes, I see you watching Jeremy and I think you might be wanting to play again. Anyway, today, a receipt fell from a pocket as I was putting your kakis into the washing machine. It is from the pawnshop in Midtown. We've walked past it so many times and the most you ever showed any interest in were the drums they have for sale. The congas. But here is a receipt for your mother's ivory broach made with 24 kt. gold that is worth so much. You pawned it. Why? What in the world would you need all this money for? Again, most women would confront you. But I won't. I have my reasons and believe me, they aren't completely selfless. I am selfish, too. I simply do not confront you because I need time. I need space to deal with this inside of me before we can deal with it together. I do not want to put something out there that can never be taken back. I need to choose who I am, what I can stand, what I want for the future. I have choices. I can go for days, weeks holding things in. Unlike you when you are upset. You know how you say things that bother you and you have been exploding lately, your comments bubbling up at me outside your heart like a skin rash—unable to be concealed.

You still coach the boys' teams. You still sleep beside me. You still bring me coffee and buy me my tulips. But, do not for a moment think I haven't noticed when you answer your cell phone and go out into the hallway and pace back and forth before you move down the elevator and into the front of the apartment building. I watch you in denial. Is it work, Jerod?

Or, someone else?

Jeremy bustles around in his room, finds the sheet music, gives me a peck on the cheek and leaves. Boys are so innocent, aren't they? Jeremy is 13 now and he still has that charming boyish naïveté. A bit like Jerod, but more in proportion to his age. I know the harder part is coming. The friends drinking, the drugs, the houses with parents out and kids alone. I have heard about it from so many friends. And the worst part: his separating. His being quiet. His not telling me things. The worst parts will be painful for him and for us. And for Justin who will miss his brother the way he used to be.

There is a change. I am afraid to be hopeful but it has been over a month now and you are finally acting more like your old self. We have had peace for a few days. You even noticed my haircut. Something is changed in you. Something big. I am wearing my melon lipstick and you even mentioned that. I love this color because it is unusual. It reminds me of my Nana. Tempest has an aunt she loved, too. All children should have a Nana. My nana had shoes to match her lip color. I wear melon now because it is who I am from my Nana down to me. Children need Nanas, don't they? I was so lucky; she would do anything for me. Coloring was one of our favorite past times. We'd color with pointy crayons for hours.

You have disentangled yourself from "her" now. You are coming back. You are laughing about something Justin did this morning. He shaved off a tiny part of one of his eyebrows because he wanted to experiment with your electric razor. Remember when he cut his bangs so short like Jim Carey in <u>Dumb and Dumber</u>? We laughed until our sides hurt.

Haven

US

Chapter 9

DAY #7 of Jerod being gone.

By: Haven

Dear Tempest:

What I really want is to have "us" back the way it used to be. I hear time heals all wounds. Can this one be healed? Was it my humming Nana that finally helped us? Maybe she finally did her work as my guardian angel.

Justin has never been musical. He is artistic with drawing. I love his artwork. Even at an early age he has shown a certain wisdom in his art. "A knowing eye," Jerod called it. He is not a teen yet. Thirteen is the turning point, and thank God I have three years left with him. I was thinking just that when I heard the knock on the apartment front door. It was soft at first and then a bit louder. I was thinking how the building's front door usually locks automatically and normally someone buzzes before being let inside the building. But there it was again; now a persistent, strong knock. My heart races. Could it be Jerod? Perhaps he has no key. How lame and non-sensible my thoughts are at this point.

I head toward the door anxiously. Oh hell, who could it be but a neighbor? I swing it open. A nice looking young man, around 35, with sandy blonde hair is standing there. He is wearing jeans, a nice button down shirt and a man purse over his shoulder. He could be a graduate student or a teaching assistant at some university like Columbia.

"Mrs. Rodriquez?" I nod.

"May I help you?" I am frightened.

Who is this man?

"I hope so. My name is Joseph. Joseph Gemignani. I am Sophia's husband." I stare at him for so long in such a stoic state that I could have won a statue contest. Finally, I utter a response. "Sophia. Sophia had a husband?" For some reason this had never even occurred to me. Sophia was married? He was still looking through my eyes and right into what little Aries Puerto Rican soul was still sound. "May I please come in? I would like to talk to you."

I nod, opening the door wider; he steps into the foyer, then stands politely waiting for more direction. "You can put your, uh, purse, on the rack there if you like," I nodded at the bamboo hat rack Jerod had carried home from the Union Square Antique Mall two years ago. The suede man purse that was around Joseph's left shoulder and hanging in front of him bandolier style was expensive looking. "That's okay, there are some things I want to show you in here. Can we just go somewhere and sit down? Somewhere private?" He looks over my shoulder into my living room, at our olive green suede couch then toward our strange pillow chair. I glance at the clock. 2 pm. I still have an hour and a half before my neighbor Cynthia would be bringing the boys home. "Of course. Follow me. Would you like anything? I have water. I have... uh, water and coffee. Um – pardon me for staring. I just never figured she was married."

"Well she was. I mean, she is. And she's gone," he stammers. I close my eyes then and picture Joseph and her. I picture them making love. I feel overwhelmed by this woman who has now conquered two men and probably more.

The woman made of deceit. The woman who creates chaos. The woman who has ruined so much.

Haven

IT TAKES A THIEF

Chapter 10

DAY #8 of Jerod's disappearance

By: Haven

Dear, dear Tempest,

I am home now. It is Day #8 of Jerod being gone and I haven't been completely honest with you. Por favor, lo siento. You see, last year when Jerod and Sophia were together, I did notice he was off in another world. But, I thought it was work. Still, deep, deep down there was a small question mark that it could be an affair. Then, one night when I was worried, I went to his office to make sure he was all right. He told me he had to work late. The kids thought I was going for a long walk. It was a lovely evening. But, when I arrived, the only ones there were the cleaners. It was 8 o'clock. I had met them before, a married couple in their 50's who live in Queens; their names are Jose and Marisol. They nodded when I explained to them Jerod had forgotten something in his office. Then, making sure they were occupied in the bathrooms with mopping the floors, I snuck around. I was so surprised to find doors, desks and drawers unlocked in the inner offices of the Tariks. It was no surprise because these three are so arrogant, they would never even suspect they might get caught.

And that is when I found files on clients that all looked the same. Every single spreadsheet looked identical with the same gains and losses, profits and loss figures. How could that be? I quickly made some copies on the machine in the hallway designated for all the offices. I was careful not to scan anything because I knew those remain there on record. I mean really! I could tell after an hour of digging that these files were fabricated. Then I poked around Jerod's office a bit. His things were in order and appeared on the up and up. As I figured, he was well in touch and meticulous with being a manager of funds in the sense of communicating with clients, keeping records in order, etc. But, Jerod was keeping up on communicating fake information to those clients. Didn't he see that? I don't know if Jerod knew at that point that their investors were being duped. He always told me I was more cynical than he was. That may be true, but this was so immediately obvious to me. If I saw this in only one visit to the files, surely Jerod knew about it. Maybe he was in the process of reporting it; or, perhaps he had been threatened if he told.

 I left with the copied documents folded inside of my purse wondering what I would do next. That was months ago and now I am wondering if what I did that night has something to do with Jerod being gone now. Pendejo! The other part I have hardly brought up again is that on the night I went to his office, Jerod was not where he said he would be. He was simply not there. I was mad as hell that Jerod had lied to me that night; my vindictive side was already kicking in. I wasn't sure how it would play out, this vindictiveness. I didn't want to kill anyone. I stole two million dollars from the Tariks in someone else's name that night. I made the spreadsheet look like all the others, but I found and attached real account numbers within the fake ledger. It was so easy. Would anyone catch it? Even if they did, they would never catch me. There were no cameras. And Jose and Marisol, being Puerto Rican like me, they didn't tell. I remember your dad, Dolphin Dad, used to say anger was sometimes a good thing. Well, that night I was angry. I did things I never would have normally done. But now I am glad I did them. Do you ever feel as though you are on the outside looking in? Like I do? Now I have these secrets and I am on the outside looking in.

The day he knocked on my door, Sophia's husband Joseph explained to me all about his marriage. He told me how at first they were very happy. Then, they had all sorts of disappointments because they couldn't have kids. Next, he lost his job at an investment firm; that, Joseph whispered, was when she started to act different. Finally, they tried being foster parents to see if adopting a child might be a way to save their marriage. But, Sophia was simply too selfish for parenting. Joseph said that soon after losing his job, Sophia met Canan at the gym and although he has no proof, he thinks Canan hired Sophia to seduce Jerod. This gave me more fuel for my "Turkey" connection.

He spoke about all this as if he was talking about going to the store to buy some milk. Joseph continued in his matter of fact manner: Sophia had latched onto working for Canan, agreeing to flirt with Jerod and just going wherever that took her. He had found a contract between them! Next, he showed me pictures of her and Jerod. At the park. At a café. At the Strand Bookstore. He had followed her one day and had taken photos of the two of them entering a small hotel in the village. Like the private detective did for Richard Gere in <u>Unfaithful</u> when he took pictures of Diane Lane and her young Italian lover. Except in this case it was Joseph who snuck around, watching his wife and her lover at the Washington Square Hotel. You could almost see the arch from their bedroom, I imagined, as I also imagined the negligee she wore. He stumbled over his words as he pulled the pictures out of his bag. All I could think about was her negligee. Made in Italy. Just like the Italian purse Jerod had bought for me once when we first got married before our money went to strollers and private school tuition. As our money went to family needs, intensity with one another had sizzled. My eyes must have been glazed over because he suddenly stopped. Joseph stumbled over the words: "Are you okay, Mrs. Rodriquez?"

I shook my head.

"No, of course I am not okay. It's the negligee. Is it dark green or black? I can't tell." I shut out all light and I closed my eyes. He looked at his photos carefully. "There is no picture of Sophia in a negligee, Mrs. Rodriquez." I opened my eyes. "Of course there isn't." He reached out and put his hand over mine. No wedding ring. He had already let go. Then, he showed me the things Jerod had gotten from her that perhaps he hadn't accepted because after all, they were here in Joseph's bag. "Gifts for Jerod," I labeled them in my head. It could be a title. Of what? A song? A movie? My life? Gifts for Jerod."

To him, my husband, from her.

There was a silver ring. And, a watch. "I gave him a watch once. How could he have accepted one from her knowing that?" I asked this by accident, out loud. "I really don't know, Mrs. Rodriquez. I didn't come here to torture you with details of their relationship. I just thought we should put our heads together and try to figure out where my wife and your husband are."

I nodded. "Haven. Call me Haven." Then, I whispered, "You know, Jerod is gone, too." He nodded his head slowly and looked out the window where Nana was spinning, listening to our every word. Her humming had gotten quite loud and disruptive because I was ignoring her. I had to. It was getting bothersome and it revealed how co-dependent we are, Nana and me.

"You have a hummingbird outside your window. There must be a feeder nearby. It stays there for a long time." He chuckled. "God, it's noisy." I cleared my throat before admitting: "Yes, that's my deceased aunt. She came back as a bird." I smiled. At first he looked at me like I was nuts, but then he cocked his head to the side and nodded. "I see. I think I understand what you mean. She didn't want to leave. She's one of those in-betweens... like in The Sixth Sense." I nod, fighting tears. "They could be together," I whisper. "Your wife and my husband." "Yes, they could be. Actually, they probably are," he looked deeply into my eyes. His eyes showed a sea of his own secrets. "Why?" I asked softly so only he could hear me as I answered my own question. "Because complacency is a sin. What you lose by being too complacent can get lost forever." Now it was Joseph who had eyes brimming with tears. I reached out and I pulled him to me. We held one another. We stayed like that for a long time.

Our pain was the same.

Tempest, I never really told you the details of how Jerod confessed the affair. He waited until the kids were at school and he sat next to me on the couch in the living room. My stomach was already turning inside out. I held my hands together on my lap and I was perspiring. On the table next to the sofa is a photograph of the four of us from a trip to Boston last Thanksgiving. Just before "*her.*" We look happy in the photo. Our colors blend and we look healthy. Like a Christmas portrait but without the red and green on. I remember we had driven up to Cape Cod and walked on the beach and taken a trolley around the town. Jerod promised me that one summer we could vacation there on the Cape. But now I ask myself, did he mean it? I hold the frame up to my nose and stare at him. It gets foggy I am breathing on it so close. I stare into Jerod's eyes as small as they are in this tiny 4 by 6 photo. I reflect on the day he did one of the most difficult things he has ever had to do. Apologize to me.

In the photo Jerod looks happy. Was I happy?

I recall that on the next day, after we got home from the Cape, we saw in the news there was a murder in that little town. It was close to where the photograph had been taken. The murder was committed by a crazed woman on meth. She had a gun, went up to a cute house where a family was on vacation. A young mother answered the door. She was wearing a blue and white nautical striped shirt; she had wanted to look like a person who goes sailing even though she didn't. You know, like Jackie Onassis in the oldest photos from before John got shot and his brains leaked out onto her lap in the convertible in Dallas.

The crazy drugged out lady put the gun up to this young mother's forehead and shot it at point blank range. She lived, but a piece of her brain went away just like John's did, and the person she was before disappeared somewhere inside her own pastel clouds. I just want my husband back alive. Those kids will never get their mom back; at least not the mom they once had. But, we still have a chance.

But back to the day he told me... Jerod defensively barked at me, that day on the sofa, that it happened because I was preoccupied with the kids. But I think it was more. I think things were bad at work and he felt frustrated and vulnerable. Aihyan had just also been hired and maybe Jerod felt threatened. He never said so, but I picked up on it. Plus, it is true; I am tired. I was tired. I sometimes feel as if I just work, work, work. These boys are a handful. But inside I know another reason he did it.

He wanted to be young and romantic again. He wanted to kiss someone new. He wanted, he wanted, he wanted.

We were wanting different things, it seems.

Why does her name have to be "Sophia," like the actress Sophia Loren whose body only seasons with age? Christ! Have you seen her in <u>Tortilla Soup</u>? Talk about hurting me in all the right spots. He met her at work; she was down the hall on a temp job, he told me with his head hanging, his hair falling into his eyes. I reached up and brushed his hair away so I could see into them. They were set in guilt. He continued, "that 'chemistry' was there from our first brush in the elevator," and then he went on, quietly explaining. I couldn't listen. I was in shock. I thought about our wedding while he spoke. I thought about a time we took the kids to the Bahamas. I thought about my father's last birthday before he died. As he divulged details because he wanted to get it off his chest, now, because I was so hurt and so appalled, I cannot recall anything else he said to me.

There is one question I never asked him. "Did you love her?"

Jerod was so remorseful. He apologized every night before we fell asleep for the year before he went missing. He bought me a beautiful new soft water pearl necklace I had been admiring for years. I knew he felt horrible. When lovers fight, or break up, or get back together, no one else knows the whole story. I do know our whole story and I know Jerod wasn't the only one at fault. He was sorry. So was I.

I have to stop dwelling on the bad stuff so I can move ahead.

I decide to do my own research about Canan and subscribe first to an online identity search online company. I pay $60 bucks to find out if she has a criminal background. It'll be even more to do an international search. I am so broke with Jerod gone and no access to his savings, no paychecks coming in for him; I am at a loss. My pay is barely enough to get us by. The Tariks say they will activate some sort of severance fund if Jerod remains missing, but so far nothing has happened. They haven't helped at all. I have never trusted them. Jerod did; that is part of his charm. Trust. And what about life insurance; if he is never found, will I get to collect that? If ever? What a mess. I look outside at the shimmering, muted reds and greens and soft crème colors left over from Christmas that reflect off of the snow laden sidewalk. I love Chelsea. I love Christmas season. High Line Park is my place now. I go and stretch out on one of their new teak chaise lounges, wrap myself up in my warm wool coat, and close my eyes under New York's sunshine. I remember, again, in misery, the days last year just before and after Christmas when these warm colors kept going on and off and I wanted so badly for them to remain constant. "Constant as a northern star," like Joni Mitchell sang; "constant as a northern star. Just before our love got lost, you said constant as a northern star." The city has placed little trees l laden with white twinkling lights all along the Highline that stay on night and day.

Twinkling with life.

Suddenly, the day gets colder. A gray cloud lifts over me and shades me in cooler air and I breathe in and out as large wafts of steam escape my mouth. The sky above is full of clouds that move quickly over me and look fractured like my life. Like they are all broken up and racing against time. Like us. There is no grace in the air. None. Yet, time stands still at the same time and can change in a moment. Does that make any sense? You hear all the noises, see all the dirt that a bustling city creates and then, in one silent moment, looking at the skyline, or seeing the sunset over the city, the noises quiet and it is only you and the sky. That is something about New York; you can wake up any day and have absolutely no idea what the day will be like or how it might change. Even if the wind chill has nearly bitten you to the core the day before, this day could be completely different. The warm sun can overtake you and wrap itself around you and pretend it is there only for you. To warm you.

I decide I had better do the search. I have to. This Canan woman could have done something to Jerod. Is she really half way across the world as she claims to be? Is Jerod, too? The police have done all the research they can and are still searching like mad. They claim they have exhausted every avenue they can think of. But I feel like there may be something they aren't telling me. In the movies and on television, the cops hold out. Is the NYPD actually holding out on me?

It takes a few minutes. Finally, the little round thing stops spinning, and there it is, her address in Turkey. Then, something else, a criminal record. I lean in ferociously, a record for embezzlement of an insurance company she worked for. She served 4 years in a prison in rural Turkey! I lean back. Wow. The lady who had come over and knocked on the door with Chai tea for me when she first moved in had been in a state prison across the world for stealing someone else's money. And we never knew.

I try to retrace my memory of Canan; for example, I try to recall when we first met, and how the kids acted with her. Kids usually sense good and evil, like dogs do. They know who is real and who is not. The boys never really took to her. But Jerod did. We had helped her when a rainstorm had caused a leak in one of her windows and the apartment manager was out of town. Then, another time, she had locked herself out of her car in Midtown and Jerod rushed up to help her with a hanger sticking out of his pea coat pocket. I thought we were just being the good neighbors and now I am wondering, was I the foolish, gullible wife next door? Then there was the time she returned Jerod's cell phone claiming she found it in the hallway. Had she stolen his phone ? Now I wonder..

Then, another time, we had dinner there. It was the night before Jerod went missing and I left my purse at her place by accident. I didn't even notice when we got home, but the next day I did notice. On my way in the hall to go get it, she was holding it on her arm getting out of the elevator. Where had she gone with my purse? She looked up, surprised, "I was just coming over to return this." I thought it strange she was getting out of the elevator with my purse. Where had she gone with it? Why hadn't she returned it the night before? I must have looked doubtful, as she glanced at it on her arm and laughed, "Oh, I went downstairs to see about the paper before I knocked on your door. I worried it might be too early." I smiled as she handed it to me. I acted as if I trusted her. But I didn't. "Oh, it's fine, I just needed to get some cash to give the boys for the subway. No problem." After she turned and left, I shut the door, ran inside, and rushed to the dining room table. I looked inside and everything was there, most in the same places; but one thing was different. My license was in a different slot. It was just one little slot over from the other cards, but I noticed. Why had she moved it? Next, I poured my coffee and stared at the boys having their cereal. I watched Jerod straighten his tie. I stared out the window at the skyline over the Hudson in the distance. And I felt scared. Scared of what was to come. Why had she moved my license? There we go again. One little damn thing messed up and I knew it could mean so much. Jerod had left me with this legacy now, full of fear and angst. Damn it.

"Jerod, I was wondering about Canan," I spoke softly. He nodded, acting uninterested. I continued, "Something about her, I don't trust her. She just acted strangely in the hallway." He came over and kissed my forehead and whispered, "She is strange, Haven. Most people are. I have to run. We are closing that big account today. I have tons of paperwork to do. Huge." Jeremy looked over toward us with that people smart look he can have. He heard the worry in my voice. He poured some orange juice and handed it to me. I looked over at Jerod. Jerod was so handsome when he was happy. I chalked it up to business success and felt relieved. I nodded. We hadn't talked about Sophia in months; he preferred it that way. Of course he did. But so did I.

They all scurried out at the same time. I got up and refilled my cup he had gotten for me on sale at Starbuck's that last week, and I looked out the window down onto the sidewalk. The three of them paced off together down the boulevard for the subway. My three guys. The boys were so smart already with New York transportation. Jerod had made sure of that. But then, wait. Canan was there, at the corner and she stopped them. She was saying something to Jerod and they were so close to one another. I perched there on my toes, looking out the window like a seagull poised to dive for food. I couldn't miss a beat. The boys were looking around, impatient to keep going. Then, Jerod nodded at her, and they departed. What had he nodded about? Canan glanced up in my direction and I spun away from the curtain fast. She couldn't have seen me. Could she have? I am so far away. What the hell? What could they have discussed? Anything at all. Damn her.

Why do women hurt each other? Are we so needy that we have to steal from one another?

By the way, nothing is easy. Being married isn't so easy. And suddenly like ice water on a hot, humid New York day, that was the moment it came over me as I pondered while looking out the window in the direction of that same corner where they had stood together. The Tariks are Turkish Americans. Did Canan know them? Did Canan know Aihyan? I scratch out these questions and I call Jack. (By the way, Tempest, thanks again for sharing your private eye. He is one in a million.) Surely, this was too much of a coincidence. After a long pondering silence, Jack asks me only one question when I tell him my thoughts. "Do Sophia and Canan know each other?" I look out the window again. Now we had the connection. We had connected Sophia to Canan, Canan to Aihyan; in fact, all of them to the Tariks. The corner was quiet, strangers bustling past. I imagined Jerod there with the boys waiting to cross the street, like ghosts from our past. The ghosts disappeared then, just like Jerod disappeared that day.

I should have confronted Canan and shaken my finger in her face and yelled something in a like, "You stay away from my husband!" I bite my fingernails and stretch my toes out in front of me. My eyebrows furrow and my stomach growls. I go sit in the living room and look over the new ads that came in the Sunday paper. I study the movie section. There are some good choices at the Lincoln Plaza Theatres.

How can I even be thinking about a movie? I feel so guilty. But what am I supposed to do all the time? Just sit here and feel sick to my stomach constantly while thinking about Jerod?

I have a secret.

I had a dream last night. Tony, my old boyfriend from high school, and Joseph Gemignani converged together and I kissed him, but he was just one man. One ideal man! Harrison Ford walked in and was jealous of my kissing this concoction of a male. I read somewhere your dreams are the secret to your soul. Is that true? Was this a past secret of my soul or a future one? Whichever it is, I hope I have it again.

I decide to take a walk to work off my anxiety. I head out toward Central Park. It is another of my favorite places to go. No matter what. I park myself across from the closed down stunning Tavern on the Green and close my eyes. It is a bit cold out, but being here fills my heart with warmth. Jerod took me here for our 10th anniversary. He gave me diamond earrings in the shape of little hearts. I was so touched. I walk home quickly deciding to wear those earrings until Jerod comes home. My face is blushing with the wind. My eyes burn as I am remembering the night with the earrings.

We were so much younger then...

My heart beats faster and as I turn my key in my door and hear the ring of the elevator that tells me someone is getting out, on our floor, right across from our door. Could it be Canan? I do nothing. I stay still pretending to fumble for something. But no, the footsteps rumble hurriedly past our door like in a war movie where Matt Damon is rushing across a barren town with blown out buildings before he hides. I feel like I am living inside a Hitchcock movie with dark shadows everywhere around me. Chris Cooper is staring at me and telling me something from his <u>Breach</u> character. That complicated, religiously torn, guilt ridden character of tragic proportion. Dark shadows grow all around me. I step into my apartment breathless.

So, my friend, that is the story of the last time I saw my husband. Out the window while I stared at him on the corner eight days ago, me feeling like that seagull, him standing too close to Canan. How I wish I could turn back the clock to that moment. How I wish I had confronted her. How I wish I had walked with them to the corner.

Two days from hell passed after that. Of course, when he never came home from work, and then by midnight when he was still not home, we had to call the cops and they were everywhere. The Tariks' other employees kept calling; Jerod's family was now stationed at our apartment with Amber. I was irritated with all the people crowding in my living room. Things cluttered the coffee table. All I could do was think of the black thong I had found in the dryer. It was stuck to the bottom. But we do live in a N.Y. apartment and we do share a laundry facility; it could have been someone else's. Yet, I couldn't get it out of my mind that they were Sophia's. They would fit her. So, that has been my life up until now. Including my short jail time. And, as you can imagine, I am going insane. Those 72 hours wasted while I sat in the damn jail cell trying to piece it altogether. Precious time. Oh, and did I mention this part? New, stronger evidence against the brothers: Major discrepancies with accounts. Everything is falling apart now.

I need to think.

Maybe I should see a psychic right away like you did. Or, maybe I need to go to confession even though I haven't been in twenty years. I think I will stick to the psychic idea. But here in New York there are so many damn psychics. How do I choose? Amber knows it all. She has been married three times, has changed careers five times. Surely, she will know of a good psychic.

And, my friends and family will all think I am nuts for paying to see one. So, of course, they will never know. That will be another one of my secrets.

Ay dios mio.

Amber has left the boys at school and I am waiting for her at a diner near 60th. She finally bustles into the restaurant, concern and discretion lining her pretty blue eyes, like a hidden cove in Hawaii. That kind of blue. That kind of hiding. Unbelievable. She is wearing a shawl that only she can pull off. It matches her eyes and she has on jeans and a pretty light yellow blouse. "Oh my God, you poor thing. This again? That bastard! What the hell is going on? I swear, men!" I am speechless. "No, Amber, He could be hurt. I don't think he would do *that* again, I swear. I think he is in trouble. I really do."

Then, I tell all; I tell her even more than I had told her in the past. I order soup hoping it will soothe me. She listens, constantly blinking in sad acknowledgement of my pain. I reveal my deepest secrets as I tell her intimate details about Jerod and Sophia. She hardly eats. She says our conversation has upset her stomach too much. I nod. Shouldn't I be the one too upset to eat? That hardly ever happens to me. I finish my lobster bisque, feeling somewhat full and contented for the first time in a long while. I remember my dad and how he cooked for us, soup and arroz con pollo on a wintry day, and I am missing him and his cooking. I am ready to look at the list of psychics she has brought. She has brought reviews on them. One is exactly in the area where I had once lived with Nana, a place where twenty years ago I was afraid to walk at night. Her name is Olga and she works out of her apartment on Clinton Street. Then there is Simone in the village on Bleeker where the young N.Y.U. students gather to study and drink coffee, scurry about to study groups and last minute plays for ten dollars. (This is the area in the movie, <u>No Reservations</u> starring Cathrine Zeta Jones) How lucky those kids are without a care in the world for what comes after graduation, yet. Then, Soho, with its trendy stores, hip restaurants and the best and newest music clubs anywhere. You can walk down almost any street and be anonymous. What a lovely way to feel. Next, Hilary in Hell's Kitchen, a stretch of area between Chelsea and Lincoln Center where you can veer off almost any avenue to a good restaurant. I would love to go and meet them all. Then, Amber suggests we get some straws from the kitchen, cut them different lengths, and choose one by the shortest draw. The shortest is Simone, the middle one is Hilary and the longest, Olga. Selfishly, I still like Olga, it is a pretty Latin name, after all. But Simone is it, so I let Amber lead. I want to have some answers and right now I will do anything to get them. Amber calls Simone and sets up an appointment swiftly.

Simone in the village.

We take the A and it goes straight there. We get off at Bleeker and her apartment, which serves as her office as well. I think about how high rents are here. It is cold out, twenty-eight degrees, and the lights from the holidays are starting to disappear and I am beyond depressed. We go to the three story walk up and I press the buzzer that has a little piece of tape on it with her name and zodiac signs surrounding it. I hope she can help me.

Simone answers, "Yes? It's Simone," But she pronounces it, "Simannnnn," and her voice is sultry and sexy. I see Amber raise an interested eyebrow. Oh, did I mention Amber is a lesbian? Between Amber and me, there is some very serious interest in what is behind the sound of Simone's voice. She buzzes our entry and we push open the glass door framed in weathered white wood from the 1920s. I sometimes wish we lived in the village; the Beat generation made its mark on this enclave of New York and even though it had become gentrified, it still holds its charm. I love Washington Square Park and right across the street, Washington Square Hotel. That hotel has been there forever, and the bar is famous in New York history. Your own father, Dolphin Dad, grew up around there. *And, Jerod slept with Sophia here.*

We start up the wide staircase that is unusual in these old places. I am in the lead. On the top floor she stands waiting wearing a long flowing, satin coral colored gown with matching slippers. Her hair is long and silver colored; it belies how young her face is. I see no wrinkles. I look closer. How is that possible? Nothing like your psychic, she seems at ease and soft. She takes my hand, then stands rubbing it as Amber reaches the landing.

"You are in so much pain. You poor thing." Then she turns to exotic Amber and smiles. "And you, what a dear friend you are. Haven truly needs you. May God bless you and keep you in your kindness and goodness." Amber looks genuinely touched and she blushes a bit before casting her cove eyes down. "Follow," whispers Simone. We did. We would have followed her anywhere. She had us hooked as soon as she answered the doorbell. We got to her door, the third on the left. She had painted it a beautiful mustard color with an old crystal doorknob accenting its charm. As we enter, I see him immediately. Your dad. He is in his customary lavender color and so distinguished looking. But he isn't a dolphin right now. No, he is in a suit and he is 40, when he was his most handome, and he is wearing those black journalist glasses you mention in your book. He nods to me in fatherly support even though he isn't my father. I understand he is here for you, for his daughter. He doesn't want you getting into any sort of trouble from helping me. I nod to him to tell him I understand. I am a parent, too. One never stops being a parent no matter how old your children become.

Simone is watching me. "Who do you see? Is it the cute dolphin man? He's been waiting all day. He got salt water on my carpet when he first arrived; it was during his change over from dolphin to man spirit, but he is such a nice man. He is Scorpio. Did you know? He wants to talk to you." She turned around to look, but he was already gone. "Oh, well I guess he and your hummingbird have now communicated because he's gone. By the way, that bird keeps checking in and she isn't so patient. Oh, Haven, you really need to tell her there are other clues as well; they are about Italy." She pauses. "It's Italian. Something about the language, but it's confusing; it is about language, but then it isn't." She shakes her head as if to rid it of the confusing parts. Then she reaches out and touches my shoulder. "Haven. Who is Joseph? The name Joseph keeps coming to me." I shrug my shoulders and bend my head looking as if I am pondering; but, truly, it is to be alone...inside my own head with yet another of my Aries secrets. I hadn't mentioned Joseph to Amber.

Suddenly, Simone sits down on her red velvet sofa looking upset. Tears run down her face like they are bursting forth from a broken faucet. Her hands are wet and when she touches the sofa, the material darkens from the moisture. Amber looks at me with questioning eyes. We aren't sure what to do next, when a cold draft fills the air.

Simone looks up with her tear stained face. "It's Jerod. He is here, Haven. He says you have never really understood him. *Who is Joseph?*"

My mind races in my Aries way. Jerod used to say that to me and it tore me to pieces. How could she know? And Italian. Of course, it is Sophia's first language. What is up with everything Italian? Creepo loved Italian food but Creepo was *your* villain! Besides, she is dead. Simone knows about Joseph! Jerod, I promise you, I will never be complacent again.

"Also, something is coming to me about a key and that you need to search the chair. But, that isn't coming from him. It is coming from somewhere else. Oh Haven, this is so baffling. What is going on?"

I wait, but Simone shakes her head at me unable to speak. She waves us away and we do not have any choice but to prepare to go. I look around the apartment, the windows are closed and the heat is on, yet cold is chilling me to the bones. I squint beyond Simone now; I see a cell, a jail cell with black iron bars and a woman and two men are there, facing the other way and I reach out. They are dark shadows, but one is Jerod's height and build. It all disappears so fast. Jerod disappears.

They reappear and Jerod turns around and reaches a hand toward me. I look into his face. For a second, he is close enough to touch. He looks so old. Mis Dios—life has beaten him up. He looks battered, bewildered. Where is he?

We put the 80 bucks in four 20s on the small glass coffee table in front of her and we stand with me still crying, her still crying, sitting on the red velvet. She calls out to us between sniffles, "He loves you with all his heart."

She waves us away. She is emotionally spent. We let ourselves out. Amber gasps, "That was weird. But it felt real. God, Haven, after this your name should be heaven. You deserve a little bit of heaven." Amber bundles her Tahiti Ocean colored scarf around her neck tightly. "Jerod could be in real trouble. I sort of believe her, don't you?" I am already bounding down the steps for the street. Of course I believe her. I saw him! It is my husband, my best friend, for Christ's sake! I hail a taxi and hop in, impatient for Amber to follow. "I need to check chairs. Which chairs?" She follows, silent. For some reason I think of candles at the Catholic church my dad used to take us to. I wish I had lit candles for Jerod there. When I was a child, lighting candles gave me hope, and warmth, and something to believe in. I loved it when the wicks would first light up larger than life and turn to a flickering flame. Right now Jerod had been larger than life before he turned to a small, flickering flame.

Now what? Do I call you? Do I call the cops again? Do I tell anyone else Joseph came to see me? The cops are finally treating it as a missing person case; but, even they are starting to see it is pretty obvious there is much more of a connection to Tariks, Inc. than any of us initially thought. The sun is setting and the boys will be home soon. I should hurry. I am going to have to call and update Jerod's mother, his boss, his sister. I have procrastinated that and will hate every minute. It has been 10 days and 6 hours now and no word. But first, I decide, I will call you. You and Mario will be here soon!

I wish I could relive and change those moments of my life before I stabbed Canan. BeforeI was arrested. Before I became completely and utterly crazy, before I was another woman inside my body.

Remember that famous actress's boyfriend who took off on a boat and never came back? Was it Olivia Newton John? I think so. But, the Olivia Newton John I want to remember is the sweet sixteen year old in <u>Grease</u>. She was innocent then. She wasn't older with a husband who leaves and causes an international media hoopla and embarrasses her because he ran away to start a new anonymous life in Mexico. It proves we all have battle scars. I am thinking all this as I ride home from Simone's sitting beside Amber in her beautiful scarf that matches her turquoise colored eyes, Simone's final words in my head, "He loves you with all his heart."

Amber gets out of the cab in Midtown to return to work; she squeezes my hand, then blows a kiss at me from the sidewalk. I lean back against the fake black vinyl/leather seat of the one millionth cab in New York City, and reflect on the dream that changes ever so slightly nightly.

MY DREAM:

Jerod is sitting in a room, a dark room. His hands are shackled to the posts of the bed. His feet are shackled as well. Canan comes in and pours water into his mouth and he almost drowns in it choking because she won't stop for him to take a breath. Her hair is as it has always been, spiked short. Suddenly a tall man comes in and places his hand around Jerod's throat, now wet from the water, choking him. He demands, "Where's the rest of the money?" Jerod remains quiet. Then he continues, "If you don't tell us, we will kill your wife and children." Jerod replies, "That is okay. They never really understood me."

Something else. Simone had said "Italian." It occurred to me to call some language schools. Maybe Sophia taught Italian. When I got home, I called all over Manhattan. I asked for instructors' names. Bingo. Sophia Gemignani works at the Linghe School of Language in Mid Town and is listed under "Faculty" on their website. "But," the man spoke softly, somewhat regretfully, "She isn't here this session. She is traveling." "Oh, too bad," I replied. I hung up and called Jack. "Good work," he said. "I will follow up. She could be traveling right in your backyard." I whispered back, "She could be traveling with my husband right in my backyard." "Yes," Jack mumbled.

Today as I feel the rain on my hair and in my face, it is so unexpected, this rain, like you and Sophia, you and these people I do not know; I wonder what was it all for? It is strange this rain, warm, almost like a summer's rain, and it is pouring in big drops like the kind that falls in Puerto Rico. The weatherman keeps saying it is breaking a record. You broke a record, too, Jerod. Our record.

I check my mail. There is an anonymous envelope postmarked from Turkey. It is marked airmail. I open it, tearing the envelope apart. There is no heading, no "Dear so and so." Instead, written in pencil:

"Please contact me if you uncover any information about Jerod or Tariks, Inc. that Jerod may have told you or that is in your possession. Or, if you hear from anyone, I beg you. Please contact me. It could mean both of us living instead of dying. I believe Jerod has been set up. And, do not contact the police about this letter, Haven. If you do, it may do more harm than good." Aihyan. 212-654-0990

A New York phone number. I sit down and my chest is so heavy I cannot take a deep breath. Set up? Should I believe him? Does he secretly know I set up the facsimile account and he's trying to get me to admit guilt? Am I the main reason Jerod is gone? Is it because of *my* embezzling the Tariks? We need answers.

I retreat, again, into Jerod's home office; I search everywhere. I find something new. I find a bag in the back of the small closet that I thought had only housed suits and shoes. In it I find cards from her. Sophia love notes. Love cards. But something hits me. The dates. They correspond exactly with certain dates. "Since last December, actually." Why am I so certain I cannot even call the police with this latest bizarre note from Aihyan? Then, a receipt falls from the bag of cards. A receipt for that language school. I read it. $555.00 for a four week session of beginning Turkish! Jerod learning Turkish and signed by him last December. Oh, Jerod, how many lies you were telling. Everything hurtful all happened during those two months. I am not sure if I should be relieved or I should simply hang myself.

"Since last December, actually."

I had searched Jerod's offices and the Tariks' offices in December. I had my deep dark secrets from that night. I melt into Mr. Buster chair with the cards. I read them over and over again. They tear at my heart. Her handwriting. Her words. "I love you." I suddenly remember once when my father took me to see a movie. It was on my 11th birthday. I keep trying to remember the name of the movie, and it escapes me. But we went in his station wagon and he was listening to Latin jazz on the radio and humming along. He was so happy. He patted my shoulder. "You look so much like your mother, Haven. You really do. When you are a little older, let's look at the old photos I saved for you. You'll see. You are so much like her." I blinked back my tears, "I don't ever want to see them, papa. I don't want to see her." His mood shifted and the sadness life can be changed him in an instant. He nodded, understanding.

When Papa died we couldn't find those photos. Nana and I looked everywhere. I have always wondered if he threw them away that day on my birthday. I guess he just didn't realize that as I grew up, the one and only thing I would always want was to see anything of my mother that might explain who she was or why she left me? How I wish I could turn back that clock and nod my head when he told me he would show me those pictures one day.

Am I prolonging our pain and Jerod's suffering with my silence? This was in the N.Y. Times today:

Midtown Manhattan. Federal authorities arrested the three Tarik brothers, owners of Tarik, Inc. on Tuesday for allegedly operating a Ponzi scheme that cheated investors out of more than eighteen million. The three brothers were taken into custody by both the FBI and Internal Revenue Service agents and charged with wire fraud, mail fraud and money laundering. The FBI office in Manhattan and Manhattan Division of Finance and Corporate Securities had been investigating for at least a year in connection with their business activities at Tarik Associates Inc., which they have operated for ten years. They reportedly got people to invest in second mortgages they sold to homeowners, promising high rates of return and a security interest in the property allegedly pledged to secure the investment. Many of the investors are from New York City. According to the indictment they spent the investors' money on personal items, including cars and second homes. The Tariks' arrest occurred just after six a.m. at their various homes in the Hamptons. Investors stopped hearing from the three brothers after they sent them a letter in January, 2011 that read: "Dear investor, I sincerley regret that I have to tell you that your investments with Tarik, Inc. have no value. The current crash of the housing market has wiped out any equity. We are closing the firm and will likely file bankruptcy." The Tarik brothers along with two missing employees, Jerod Rodriquez and Aihyan Cleyet, are scheduled to be arraigned February 8th before Judge Thomas Coffin in the U.S. District Court in New York City, New York. Authorities suspect foul play.

Jeremy comes into the room, stands at the open door of the closet and sees me. He looks at me with a questioning look. I am mortified Jerod is mentioned in the article. I try to hide the cards, this article, and the letter from her. "Mom, don't worry. They'll find him. Daddy will come home. He promised to coach baseball this spring, remember?" I vow to myself, "My boys will not be hurt by these people." The phone rings, jolting me from my sad trance. When I stand, one more small photo falls from my lap. It's her. Can she never leave me alone? She is standing on a balcony with windchimes blowing in the air behind her head.

Haven

CAROLINE

Chapter 11

By: Haven

Dear Tempest:

I remember once when I was a teen; I babysat for a couple named Selby and Jeff that lived in the Upper West. He was a musician who had written songs for a couple of popular rock bands back then. One or two had big hits. They were 70's rock and roll hippies. They had long hair, cool cars, and two kids with radical 70's names like Star and Summer. They used to have dinner parties with famous people who lived in Manhattan and sometimes I would watch their kids while they were entertaining. One time it was a very famous band that had the name of a city. Was it Detroit? I forget. No. It was Portland. How could I have forgotten that? I answered the door for each of them, with their long wavy hair and beautiful women on their arms. Shelby and I took their coats and escorted them into the living room. It was something in their body language, or their voices, the two of them: Shelby, the woman I worked for, and the lead singer of Portland whose name was Vince. Somehow, instinctively, I knew they were having an affair. He handed her his coat, and it was like she had held it before. He brushed up against her when his wife went to use the restroom. They caught eyes. Then, they caught *me* catching *them*; Shelby blushed. I could feel such sadness from Shelby it overtook me. But, Tempest, you had so many wonderful souls surrounding you when Creepo did all her horrible acts. Thank God for your friend, Mr. Sunshine, tracing phone calls and other friends taking care of you, like handsome Dr. Falsett, the eye doctor who comforted you. Thank God for all your friends, Tempest. Sasha, Meghan, your mom, Gwenyth, and your family. I don't feel so close to my half siblings throughout this nightmare; instead, they are annoying me. I just want them and most everyone else to leave me alone.

Thirty-nine years ago, at fifteen, I babysat for Shelby. One month later I went over to her house again to watch the children; her husband was out of town. She answered the door and she had been crying. Back then mascara leaked so much you would look like a raccoon if you cried. The tension in the air was thick. When she said good-bye and went out the front door, a big black car picked her up; I was peeking out the window. Vince stood there holding the door open for her, he was the singer from Portland. She was on her way to have an abortion. Don't ask me how I know these things. Soon, her kids were calling out to me from the den, so I turned away from the window, but this is what I remember. I saw a child. A beautiful little girl named Caroline, she was five, and she was standing there in the walkway waving to me. I knew she was the spirit of the child Shelby was about to abort. Somehow she would be frozen in time as a child around five years of age, *never of this world.*

I still see her at times, here and there. She was never born in the human sense, but somehow she became a young life between heaven and earth and there she thrived. She latched onto me and has never left. Little Princess Caroline who was standing outside of Shelby's house. I thought of Princess Diana. I never told you before how I adored her. I don't usually get immersed in a celebrity's life. But Diana was different. Now, I think with clarity how Caroline and Diana have one another to share heaven with. It is a sweet thought.

 Haven

WHAT SHOULD I DO?

Chapter 12

By: Tempest

Where should Mario and I begin to look? It has already been a week and a half this guy has been gone and I really do not know what the N.Y. cops know. I have tried my psychic tricks, but they're coming up empty. The psychic said to look in the obvious spaces, so that is what I will do. I will go to New York and look in Jerod's obvious places where the police might not think to look. It is in the everyday steps of a person, you know. It is in the day-by-day feel of a person, how he walks, what he's thinking, the simple hellos and the quiet drives. It is in the music he listens to. Those are the places the answers are about people. But I am no detective. I am just a woman who is now free, free to love and be and write, and do water colors of the sea and finally do yoga on my violet colored mat. And locate Jerod.

"Hello?" She whimpers into the phone.

"Haven?" I speak softly. " It is Tempest calling." She pauses, "Hello Tempest. It is so good to hear your voice. Gracias." Is she sniffling? It feels like she is sniffling. Of course she is. Her life is in shambles. I am not

sure how to begin. "We all will help you, Haven. We will try." "Thank you. Thank you," she says a bit louder. Then I can see them in my mind, all four of them: the tall, dark man named Jerod with hazel eyes and generous hair around his temples. I see what she looks like, pretty as she is. The <u>Sixth Sense</u> part of me is alive and well as I see them boys so clearly. We talk a bit; I tell her I am coming to New York; we set a date. Then, we hang up. I close my eyes and I see them again: Jeremy comes up and rubs her shoulders and kisses the top of her head. Just like Jerod used to do. And outside of her bedroom window is a pretty yellow colored bird spinning its wings like crazy. Her Nana.

Then something shifts and something absolutely horrible happens. I feel myself stabbing someone. A woman. I keep my eyes closed and try to picture who it is. The air goes blank. Prison does strange things to your psyche, remember? When I opened my eyes, Mario was staring at me concerned.

"What did you see? You were shaking." I pretend I don't remember. I do not confess my visions.

Later that night, Mario shakes his head when I tell him I am really not being an accomplice to someone else's crime; rather, I am just exploring Haven's case. He says I am risking my freedom and he waited too long for it for me to do that. That he can sense I am going off into distant territory and it frightens him. I tell him I waited too long for my release, and I do not want to risk anything, including losing him, either. We are edgy with one another and this is unusual. I know he loves me and that is why. I don't deserve this man who has moved to a different part of the country for me and is so generous to me. My secret shame of the murder I committed is like a permanent cancer in my body that will never disappear. It has metastasized.

Then he kisses my hand like a gentleman from a 40's movie, like Cary Grant, and I am swept away at his vintage like romantic love for me. I can't say I love him as much as I loved Peter. I may never. But he is getting closer. He wears a soft colored tan linen shirt tonight and kakis. He dresses simply and eloquently. He is old enough to understand goodness, and he embraces it. His hair is full and brown and his shoulders are broad and strong. He isn't as tall as Peter was, but his strength is in his will and kindness, not his height. I remember when he told me he liked my eye patch back when he came over to check the lantana plants and ivy where Creepo had broken in under our house. All he said was, "I like it." Mario is one to let things go. He is easier on himself than Peter ever was. He is different and it isn't bad. But right now he is acting dominant and I don't appreciate it. I am stubborn and decide, "So be it, I will go to New York alone. But where the hell is Jerod Rodriquez?"

More from Haven is coming through on email, but I am distracted now. I am thinking about our plan, damn it. Mario and Haven, both of you, give me space. This is all relatively new to me. Having a boyfriend, for one. Being involved in private eye stuff, for two. Helping a desperate soul mate, for three. I need an Advil, oh hell; I need a glass of red wine. It has flavonoids, good for me, and it will make me relax. I need to relax. Reader, it scares me what I am about to confess to you. I need to relax, but it is not only because Haven's story is stressing me out. I need to relax because of the adrenaline running through my body at the mere thought of killing again. There, I've said it. The mere thought of killing gets me excited. I admit it.

Then there is Jack, who helped me so much with Creepo. He just isn't quite as gun-ho as I am about helping Haven; he wants to help, but he is so booked with some case in Washington D.C. dealing with a young Senator's aide who was found stuffed in a suit case that arrived at her parents' apartment. How disgusting and horrific for those parents. She had been strangled. He is the leading private investigator on the case. Finding Jerod isn't a high priority for Jack right now. Besides, Jack loves me, not Haven. Had you guessed that, dear reader? That he had a crush on me while we were searching for Creepo? He wants to help, but we are both a bit in the dark due to the nature of her relationship with Jerod. But at least they are in touch now, Jack and Haven.

I pour my wine, a Merlot from Solvang, near Santa Barbara where that movie <u>Sideways</u> was filmed. I sit on my favorite chair, pulling my throw over my cold feet; I call Jack to explore what should be my first step. We have so few clues. He tells me to listen carefully to every single thing she tells me or writes to me and to tell Haven she has to trust her instincts. He also makes me contemplate Jerod's work. Was there anything special or different about it or him regarding his work lately? Besides what I had uncovered, were there any other clues? And that is when I remember <u>Ghost,</u> the movie written by Bruce Joel Rubin. Patrick Swayze's character had worked in some investment job and his partner was embezzling the corporation and killing Patrick allowed him to do something profitable. Jack also said he *would be in New York, but only for a few days; even so, he'd meet up with us. Then, Mario and I could follow his lead. I hang up and go online to reserve a train/hotel package for us. I am so excited. It is almost the early days of spring. Little is more beautiful than early spring in New York. The train ride won't take very long, and the tracks lace through some lovely areas of New England, like a photo on a calendar. I think about Rhode Island and how I have always wanted to go see the huge mansions it is so famous for. I dream of Connecticut and remember the house that Michael Douglas and Anne Archer buy in Connecticut in <u>Fatal Attraction</u> when they move out of Manhattan with dreams of a more idyllic life; at least, that is, until Glenn Close comes along and ruins it all. Like Creepo ruined our lives. Like Sophia is ruining Haven's life. I am talking about when Glenn Close kills their daughter's bunny rabbit and boils it in a big pot for when Anne and the adorable pixie hair girl get home. It is a very disconcerting and disturbing scene. The house they moved to and the neighborhood reminds me of Portsmouth.*

Portsmouth has a lot of painful memories for me, but it also has the house Peter found for me and bought for us and I love it, the one I bought back. Isn't that strange, how pain changes? At first, every time I thought of

Peter and the yellow house with the red door, I thought I would never step foot inside. Now, I like it. I like it that we had moved here to start a new life. I like it he found the house. I like that my first time there Sarah was with us. I've managed to gloss over the worst parts of it all. I turn and look up at the hillside where Creepo spied on us, and there is nothing left but a tree. A tree the kids and I planted in Peter's memory. I smile.

She got what she deserved. She and her garlic breath.

Then, in the blink of an eye I start feeling insecure. I thank Jack and hang up, knowing he will call back with ideas that are now growing in his fertile little private eye mind. I also know I am no detective. But I can learn. I do have good instincts. I make a list. I will go to Jerod's dry-cleaner's and see if anything has been left behind. In every movie I have ever seen when a man is having an affair, something happens with a pocket in a suit from the dry cleaner's. Next, I will go to Jerod's office and ask around. I can figure something out and I will. I can pretend to be doing a survey. I have charm. I can do this. I will wander around their apartment building, even downstairs in the laundry room like in all the James Patterson or Sue Grafton novels with detectives doing their finest sleuth work.

I will go to the boys' schools and do some searching there. Maybe someone will know something Haven doesn't. I am on a roll and I make a list. Then, the phone rings and it is Mario telling me to forget the hotel/train package. Instead we are going to get a driver to take us into the city and we will stay at the Gramercy Hotel; I am beyond excited. I stop thinking about Haven, and I google The Gramercy and sit for hours poring over the history of the hotel, the neighborhood sites, and other things I want to do in New York. Selfish me.

By the way, did I mention that Haven heard from someone who had found Jerod's wallet? Some woman who works in the Bronx, at Fordham. She found it in a ditch in front of a liquor store close to campus. His money was still there; everything was in tact. She called the police and they were so shocked that no one stole anything. It had gotten covered by some twigs and leaves. That explains why the money was still inside. Maybe he threw it there hoping we would follow the trail. Jack said he would check it out. If Jerod threw it on purpose, his captors didn't notice. I tear this story apart in my mind, section by section. I pull out the cards, receipts, bills, his license. I think again of Angelina Jolie in <u>The Mighty Heart</u> *when she knows Daniel is saying something to her on his last video. I picture Jerod being driven and his sneaking his hand into his pocket; then, discreetly, he throws the wallet out the window. When the cops brought the wallet to me, at first, nothing seemed odd or out of place. Then I see it, folded up so tiny, stuck into a corner behind his license there is a receipt for a Post Office box in Soho. But then, something else, a key, wrapped tightly inside the receipt. Both stumble onto the floor. They'd been stuck deep down inside, hidden. Like Haven's secrets she thinks I don't know.*

Haven described for me how she searched every chair in their home and there was nothing. But she didn't tell me about the key. She has forgotten I see these things. Or about the names of clients she had stolen, or about the documents she copied. Those have a part in this tale. Do you remember I hear voices? I see dead people. I am more and more psychic; this part of me is more alive. And, she never mentioned Joseph. Why is she holding back so much information? I see things all the time, day and night. I hear things all the time. Like Dolphin Dad used to say to me, "You are a witch." Now that I accept it, it is more prominent. I can't escape it. And today I saw it all: the wallet, the key, Haven in the living room with Joseph.

I have a new vision. This time it is Jerod on a plane. He is blindfolded and tied to the plane seat. He is struggling to free his hands.

And then another. God! Make these images stop! I want to do the real work. The search, the investigating.

They are in her apartment, I guess... Sophia's voice has dropped to that throaty, husky sound. Jerod's voice sets her on edge. Reaching out, she grabs for the collar of his shirt. Her fingers graze his tan, warm skin.

Wait! Damn it. I want to stop these scenes! But I can't.

His stomach muscles ripple beneath her touch and he sucks in his breath. Never in her life has someone filled her with desire to this level. Her body trembles silently as she pulls her blouse up and over her head, exposing her breasts. Heat emanates from his body to hers, pulling her in, enticing her. Although instinct tells her to step back, she is drawn to him in ways she doesn't understand. Jerod lets out a gasp that reverberates inside her. She taunts him. "It's my job to make you feel better." And it was. (Yes, I was pretty sure now. She had been paid for this seduction). She leans in kissing his mouth. "Sophia," He whispers her name and it comes out sounding like both a warning and a plea. The next thing she knew everything between them was hungry. Famished. His tongue delves inside her mouth with passion, taking all she offers and giving even more. (I blush with this vision). Desire explodes and at that moment she knows.

Jerod would be the man to fill the emptiness she'd felt for so long, an ache she knows only he can satisfy. She has to have him. "You okay?" *He eyes her with a concern she craves. This man she had been paid to lure away from his family, to open up to her about other things; Jerod is the one and only man she would never give up. She nods.* "Fine. You?" *A grin curves his lips.* "Never better."

The vision fades to black.

"Mario?" I whisper. He turns towards me groggily. "I have to help Haven. I have no choice." He pulls me to him tightly.

"I know that," he whispers.

THE ACCIDENT AND THE COLOR MINT GREEN

Chapter 13

By: Tempest

An absolutely horrible thing has happened to Sarah as we were packing for New York. She was in a car accident. It was on one of those crazy freeway interchanges in Los Angeles when someone tried to cut her off; she flew over two lanes and hit a wall head on. I forgot to tell you she had moved to Boston, not long after I went to prison. But being anywhere near me and the house where Peter and I had been seemed too painful for her, so she moved far away, to the west coast. She broke her ankle trying to brake, and the seatbelt and air bag did a horrible number on her neck, collarbone and chest area. Her car is totaled. "She's okay. But she is hurt." I didn't need to hear 'her' name. I knew it was Sarah. She had never been an aggressive driver. We hurriedly arranged last minute flights for Los Angeles. Just before take off, I wrote to Haven to let her know I would be out of commission for a bit. I was so anxious; I couldn't concentrate on anything on the plane; I kept switching from television reruns and a movie I bought for two bucks. Mario fell asleep straight away. He was at peace. It isn't his daughter. She's mine and Peter's, and at that moment I missed Peter so much. I thought about all of our losses. My ten years not being with the kids. My loss of Peter forever. My loss of the woman I had been and the transformation into the monster I am now. Yes, dear reader, I am a monster now. And it's too late to turn it back.

Then the color of a light green mint came over me. When Sarah was at Georgetown, at 20, she got it into her head she wanted her room all mint green. So, of course, I was there for a visit and our focus became that color green. We went to shop for a green comforter, a little green trash can, green curtains, and green pillows. The whole nine yards. We found a store with a lamp that had the perfect mint color shade. We bought light green crystal dresser knobs from a hardware store. We climbed up and down stairs, in and out of taxis with mint green objects over flowing out of bags and over our shoulders.

Here is the thing about being a mom. You feel those damn shots they have to get every year or so when they are small. You hold back saying things to their friends who can be mean when they are in those arduous adolescent and teen years when bullying reaches an all time high. You cry just as hard when they don't get a prominent part in a play they have their hearts set on. You are on the roller coaster ride every single step of the way. Every single day.

Then they grow up.

Poor Sarah. Just as her documentary was getting funding, just as she was ready to edit, just as she found people to help her write a grant... this had to happen. My cell had a text message and it was Kyle. He wrote, "We'll be out there tomorrow."

It made my heart melt that the kids are so close that they would come out to be there for their sister, no questions asked. Peter was part of that reason. He had always been good at making sure the kids were close to each other. Parents want children who grow up and are kind and supportive of each other.

Dear reader, do you remember when Suong White's father came to see me when I got out of prison? He wanted to meet the person who had killed his daughter. As Mario and I climbed into Mario's car, he whispered something that still disturbs me. He leaned towards my open front passenger window and breathed these words, "I came to say I forgive you. But I can't." Mario closed my car window quickly from the driver's side. I had murdered his daughter who had killed my husband. I would say it deserved at least a conversation. Maybe even an apology.

IN THE MIDDLE OF ALL
OF THIS... A FUNDRAISER

Chapter 14

DAY #11 of Jerod being gone

By: Haven

Dear Tempest:

Yesterday marked Jerod's 11th day missing. One week and 4 days gone. Then I heard your horrible news about your daughter in that accident. I am very sorry.

    The police are interrogating a lot of folks more now since I have shared my suspicions about Canan. I still haven't shown them Aihyan's letter, or the key. I am not sure why, maybe woman's intuition.

    It is cold and gray out. Appropriate for my mood. There are lots of cars everywhere in the village. More cabs than ever. I rushed up here to a little vintage store that carries some things I like. I wanted to buy something for your Sarah and besides, these days I do anything to take my mind off of my life. But, by the time I got here, what I was looking for was sold out. As usual, all I can think about is Jerod anyway. I need a diversion and that is why I decide to get away for the day. I have to, or I will go absolutely nuts. If I could just be close to him, feel the warmth in his hands, look into his eyes, I would feel so much better.

Next, still feeling a surge of this undercurrent of uneasiness and trying hard to hide it, I meet Amber for lunch. I forgot to mention it is her birthday. I had almost forgotten it is her birthday, so I am overwhelmed with guilt for being a bad friend right now. We sit in a little Tuscany type village restaurant below the sidewalk and order salads with warm bread. The bread arrives in a basket with real butter that comes in little tubs. Once again, the food comforts my heartache. She drinks some wine, barely touches her salad and looks tired.

She loves the photo I brought for her of the four of us. After lunch, we had plans to go to a fundraiser for a friend's daughter who had also been in a car accident. However, in her case, she wasn't as fortunate as Sarah is. We took the subway out to Brooklyn, to a nice house in Williamsburg, and soon after I arrived, Caroline did, too.

A young trio of musicians had been asked to play. We headed toward the house, the last one in the cul de sac, the one overlooking a green field. I looked out, and the smells of life overwhelmed me which is unusual in Brooklyn, to have that outdoor scent overwhelm you. I saw a rabbit scurry over some rocks in the distance. Then I heard the music. The sounds were clear and warm. Then, much to my soulful surprise, when I looked out over the green belt, there was the lovely, familiar girl.

She blew me a kiss. Shelby's ghost baby. But wait, I reminded myself, "She never became human, yet here she is... again." I smiled. Aren't I becoming more like you now, Tempest?

I looked around at the large crowd of guests; there were a few single wanderers and the young woman that the party was honoring. She, too, looked vaguely familiar with dimples and bright blue eyes and a peppy pony tail that seemed to want to jump right off of the back of her head. She smiled at me. I instantly realized who she was. She was Katie, a girl who had gone to grammar school with my children. We had never spoken, but I remembered her, I remembered her mom, a tall, slim pretty lady with shoulder length blonde hair that used to work in the financial district and had been there on 9/11. But, she was okay. One of the lucky ones. And I recalled then that she had a little sister, more hyper than Katie, the little pistol of the family. I remembered them from church, the side chapel. Katie, her little sister and her folks were a foursome, loyal to the school, a regular family. Even then, in her little private school uniform, her pony tail bounced with life right off of the back of her head.

But here she was, at thirteen, in a wheel chair, unable to walk. This benefit, I realized with agony, was for Katie.

I walked over to a poster with all the photos of her in her graduation cap and gown from middle school, in her rehabilitation therapy sessions with nurses and aides, with her friends around her hospital bed. The photos were so much like the ones I had in an album on our coffee table at home, of Jeremy's own recent graduation from middle school. It could have been our photos on this board, only these had Katie's face and two dimples. She looked up at me and smiled. I said, "Hi Katie, I am Jeremy's mom, you might remember me? I am happy to see you. I remember you." She nodded. There was so much spoken between us that we stopped there. She remembered me, I remembered her; it was as if all of the years of walking around that school converged in recollections, the years of talent shows, of giggling, of saying the Pledge of Allegiance outside on the black top. We had seen each other millions of times. I had no idea that the Katie who had a spinal chord injury was the little Katie I had always noticed and thought was so adorable for so many years.

And now, her parents were sitting outside on Adirondack chairs at a friend's house in Williamsburg listening to people sing to raise money for their daughter.

Their eyes held such sadness that I couldn't bear to look at them. I couldn't bear to speak with them.

I wandered over to a stool and sat alone listening to the different songs from our generation such as "Leaving on a Jet Plane," and "Bridge over Troubled Waters." But then Katie's dad came over and stood beside me. I looked up at him. I said, "I remember you from Chelsea Academy." He nodded. I whispered, "I cannot even imagine." He replied, "That is what everyone says. And it's true. Then they ask how I am. And I forget sometimes and answer, 'I am good.' But, I'm not. I won't ever be good again until my little girl can walk." He turned and left to go inside. I looked at

Amber, "I need to leave." She nodded; we picked up our purses and pulled our coats tighter. I turned one last time to look at Katie; she was watching us leave without a good-bye. She nodded sweetly at me, her pony-tail dancing in the breeze behind her head.

Two things happened when I got home: Jack called and he had asked around in the neighborhood where Jerod's wallet was found. Someone else saw a forest green colored SUV that day. It rounded the corner where the wallet was found; a lady sweeping the sidewalk saw a man in the back seat through the open window of the car. He had dark hair and his glasses fell off. He had his arm out the window for a second, and she said the wallet could have been dropped. I got sick to my stomach. *It had to be Jerod.* He wears glasses.

Then, Amber dropped a bombshell on me on the way home from Brooklyn. She told me she is in love with me. My mouth dropped open a bit like when Joseph came over to talk to me. I could have caught a fly in it for it being open so long. "Well, just in case he never returns. You have me." I thought to myself, " I will have Amber to love me." I thought about it in a pondering, fascinated sort of way. I had never in my adult life considered loving a woman. It was an interesting idea. But, I really didn't need another thing to worry about.

Haven

NANA

Chapter 15

By: Haven

Dear Tempest:

Nana in real life loved and embraced raising my siblings and me. That is why she has never truly left. Even in death, she never left. She couldn't, as she raised me after my father died. I am sure that is why she came back humming. She wants me to know she is right here.

The noise of Nana.

The way I came to live with my nana was most unusual and in the beginning, sad. Remember, at a certain point there was no father and no biological mother – just me and Nana, Bella, Maureen, and Casey.

My mom was Nana's younger sister. She had gotten pregnant with me from my dad. They were young and impetuous, but especially my mom was. My father was a widower, already raising children from his first marriage. He came to claim me and my mother a month after I was born. Thank God he did. I never would have gotten to know him otherwise. He had deep set eyes, like I do. He was a bit precocious, like I am. He liked exercise and art, like me. My mother, Bonnie, showed up at Nana's front door on the Lower East side of Manhattan 9 months pregnant, alone, broke and needy. Nana had been married once and her husband had died of Melanoma. They had no children. Bonnie loved Nana, but she was proud and stubborn to the point of self-destruction. So, when she arrived at Nana's, pregnant, she was too proud to admit that she needed extra help from a doctor. She had been warned that she could become toxemic, and she also had been warned she was prone to placenta previa. So when she went into labor, she hadn't taken the right precautions, and a few horrible things lined up to cause hemorrhaging and she almost died. But she didn't.

When my father showed up, he begged my mother to come live with him and his three children from his first marrige; we moved to a suburb of New York. Nana was heartbroken. She saw the distance between the Lower East and Yonkers like it was a continent apart.

A few years after trying, my mom took off. She wasn't cut out for mothering. Something like in <u>Kramer</u> <u>vs.</u> <u>Kramer</u>. But, unlike Meryl Streep, my mom never returned. And, when I was eleven and a half years old and my dad was killed in a car accident, Nana stepped in to take care of me, again. This time, she took my half siblings, too, and we all moved in with her on Clinton Street. Big changes for four kids from Yonkers.

Recently, Nana passed away. But, as you and I know, she didn't go very far.

The day my dad died, the day my mama left, and the day Nana died are three moments edged in my memory forever. Jerod had come home from work first on the day Nana died. There was a message from our neighbor, Mrs. Moffett. She called to say Nana was in the hospital. She'd had a heart attack. Jerod had called me right away, but by the time I got through to the hospital it was too late. The woman who had become my mom, dad, aunt, and grandma was gone. Nana used to love to garden and cook. She never worked past her 20's, and then, once we came around she was plenty busy. And between my father's and her own husband's life insurance, she was able to take care of us. I was lucky. I was so secure in growing up with Nana, giving was natural for me. The reason I am sharing this is because of this:

I know that the love from Nana was like an extra layer of good skin, just enough to sustain me through the bad stuff.

Haven

I HAVE BEEN CALLING HER

Chapter 16

DAY #12.

By: Haven

Dear Tempest:

I understand that you cannot come to New York as we planned. Selfishly, I was so anxious to tell you in person what Simone the psychic told us. But I sense you already have this knowledge. Amber is still blown away by our psychic encounter. I am still blown away by what Amber said to me. Who wouldn't be? Justin and Jeremy keep telling me they are having a dream about their father and that he is in a room with one window high up. Isn't that strange? That they would have a similar dream to mine? I have heard of close people connecting in that way.

I haven't told them I am still dreaming a similar dream.

MY DREAM:

Jerod is either lying on a bed, tied to the bedposts, or he is sitting on cot with an undershirt on, his legs shackled to the leg of the cot. There is a single light bulb high above his bed. He looks horrible, like a prisoner of war. Emaciated. There is a scar across his forehead as if someone sliced him with a knife. Dried blood is all over him in dark patches just like how

Bruce Willis looks after fighting someone in one of the <u>Die</u> <u>Hard</u> movies. And, there is a small dvd camera set on a tripod across from him. Just like Al Queda does with prisoners. Like what happened to Daniel Pearl when all he wanted was to spread peace.

He has a beard, and his hair is horribly cut as if done with a bad scissors. His eyes have no green alive in them. They are that gray color I told you about that his uncle had in his eyes after his heart attack. I am so upset that often, in my unsteady sleep, I cry out and sit straight up. I am breathing heavily, on the verge of hyperventilating. I struggle with the details. I wonder if it is a message to me. This repetitive dream. He lies down and breathes with difficulty and looks up at the window that sheds a tiny bit of hope over him in the way a sunrise over Istanbul can.

I stop and listen to Nana's humming. I'm falling apart. I am ugly with big gray circles under my eyes. It is a good thing I am not working right now. I would never have the strength or stamina to care for my patients. I haven't worked in two weeks; usually it is my job that keeps me grounded. Amber tells me to go get a massage, to do things for myself. Instead, I stay close to the house. I worry one of the boys' teachers might call me or someone may stop by, or some news may come in, something. I need to feel connected to Jerod all the time. Being home helps me feel connected.

In case he shows up. In case they dump him here. In case he leaves her. In case he still loves me. In case he has always loved me.

In case, in case, in case.

Another reason I work in the emergency room at the hospital is because I see every level of society. Money doesn't matter with grief. No matter how much money one has, grief is the same. My job keeps me in the real world. Feeling grateful.

I picture Jerod drugged and hurt. I have been in such denial of that pain. I have been in such denial because perhaps I caused it. Nana's humming gets louder outside our window. She is humming some pretty Sinatra tune I haven't heard in a long, long time. What could it be? Then she transitions into a different one. At first, I do not recognize it. But then I remember. Of course. It is the song Jerod and I say is "our song." It is "You Send Me," by Sam Cooke. "Darling, you send me." She is trying to distract me. Nana always knows how to get to me.

A BIG SECRET OF MINE

Chapter 17

DAY #13: Jerod has been gone almost two weeks now

By: Haven

Dear Tempest:

Thirteen days. Can you even try to relate to this feeling of despair and utter uselessness? I collect my whole life into one little box, then I open it up and let out pieces of memories one by one. They sustain me through this heart ache. I have never been so miserable. Justin didn't want to go to school. I don't blame him. Still, it is better to stay occupied for the boys. I almost hyperventilated after my dream. I sometimes feel as though there is no reason to go on. Why go to the trouble when things like this happen? Torture, death, sadness.

I keep picturing you and I in a car driving over a cliff at the Grand Canyon the way <u>Thelma and Louise</u> did. I sit and watch the phone. At least I am here alone with the kids now. Others have resumed their lives, somewhat. The NY Times did a feature on the Tariks. The man who wrote the piece is investigating the Tariks on his own.

I have to calm and appease my mother-in-law. My own half siblings call constantly and I get so tired of explaining anything new to each of them. I am tired of comforting other people. I tell the kids that their dad will come home some day. I look over love letters he gave me when we first met. I know it isn't healthy, but I reread "her" letters to him. Damn her to hell. I even take out Tony's old letters and read those. Is it possible to love two men? I tell myself I do. I think I do this out of hurt. I am hurt that Jerod could have loved two women. Or did he?

Remember the days way before the Internet when people wrote love letters? When Jerod and I first met he wrote romantic letters to me. We waited so long to get married after he proposed. I feel like I have known him forever. I miss Jerod moving out of my way in the kitchen. I miss seeing him in his flannel pajamas in the mornings. I miss the smell of his subtle cologne, the one the Tariks always gave him. I miss him in the brown robe we bought one weekend when we went away to an Irish Bed and Breakfast up the coast, in Maine.

I miss when we'd go to Rockefeller Center to walk around. I know I won't marry again. I decide to go back into his email account. Then I have a radical brainstorm. Once he sent me a folder. It is on my computer desktop at the clinic. He obviously wanted me to save it! I get dressed so fast and run outside to flag down a taxi. I get to St. Mark's and almost fall out of the cab remembering the folder marked "Jerod" in my office. I rush inside calling greetings over my shoulder and sit at my cubicle. I can hardly wait for the computer to come on. There are over a hundred emails from his last days at work. But even after hours of poring over them I could see it was only research he had done about the background of his employers. The three brothers had all graduated with MBAs from Harvard. Each had special talents. They took American names so as to better blend with society. They kept their Turkish last name; Sean was a computer genius. He could create programs of any kind and quickly. IBM, Xerox, Apple—all of them tried to woo him toward their entities, but he had none of it. He followed his own beat of success and knew he could do things on his own that no one else was capable of. Then there was Clint, the middle brother. Clint was the risk taker, the bold one who loved the danger in stepping out of the comfort zone. And third was charming Blake Tarik. He was the best looking, the most well rounded. He had tried to break off ties with his brothers more than once, but they guilted him into staying. Later, he would be the first to break and tell the authorities the truth. Blake had a conscience.

In 2005, Jerod had met Blake at the gym; on treadmills beside one another. They discussed Blake's investment firm and Blake had boasted it was unlike all others. What Jerod didn't know and couldn't know was the extensive search that had gone into finding someone bright enough, idealistic enough and willing. Blake knew Jerod would be on that treadmill and he knew Jerod was the perfect target.

They had already researched Jerod. They already knew all about him and *had chosen him.*

According to Jerod, Sophia had convinced him she wasn't interested in anything serious. Jerod, guilt ridden after a short while, wanted to end it. She began calling incessantly at his office, showing up on corners near his office scaring Jerod that I might see them together. Then, she started to blackmail him by threatening to tell me about them. Jerod says he didn't want to hurt me. That's what kept him placating her. Finally, he suspected she was being paid to distract him. There couldn't have been a better way to do it. During this time, I was writing in my journals about how different he was acting. I knew he was suffering, but I was suffering, too. He had become so remote.

Bernie Madoff went on trial. Madoff pleaded guilty to eleven federal offenses, including securities and mail fraud, theft from his employee benefit plan, making false filings with the SEC and so much more. The plea was a response to a criminal complaint filed, which stated Madoff had defrauded his clients of almost sixty-five billion in the largest Ponzi scheme in history. Madoff didn't get a plea bargain with the government. Rather, he pleaded guilty to all of the charges. It has been reported that he did so because he refused to cooperate and name any conspirators.

What if I get arrested for my theft? What if I go to prison this time, like you, Tempest?

Were the Tariks guilty of something smaller yet similar? Of course I knew this answer. I was a party to their crime now. I had stolen paperwork. And dear reader, remember, I created a new file under a fake name, a fake client. I generated inter-office correspondence between Aihyan and Jerod, each not knowing this facsimile client was my creation. He,

"Mr. Schintock," invested two million dollars in the investment firm of Tariks, Inc. Aihyan changed the numbers to look like a steady monthly profit, fabricated just like the other files. Jerod thought Aihyan had taken over this particular file from the brothers, and Aihyan assumed Jerod did. So, when the office cut a profit check that was, of course, based on my lie, it was cut to my alias, "Mr. Schintock." I left no trace whatsoever. Did Jerod know anything about this?

I have over two million dollars in cash hiding. I scammed the brothers at their very own game, so they cannot report me—as that would be reporting themselves. By the way, "Mr. Schintock" resides in Puerto Rico now.

I didn't reveal my Aries secret.

Haven

FRIEND AMBER

Chapter 18

By: Haven

Dear Tempest:

When we were younger, Amber was so radical. She got a belly button ring before anyone else did. She had tattoos on her ankles long before they became popular. She took a lot of acid in college and ruined her chromosomes so much with chemical altering that she knew instinctively she should never have children. She was a Dead Head for years, following the Grateful Dead all around the west coast, up and down and down and up. For a while it was her career, life, love, and past time. She fell into all sorts of crazy situations. Amber could be an icon, an icon of the 60's. You could pluck her up from any place at any time and her stories would be stories of that era. Her guitar had bright, florescent flower stickers all over it. She had long, straight pretty hair and wore a leather fringe jacket everywhere, even in warm weather. Even now she pulls that coat out and wears it once in a while.

Amber had that Woodstock feel to her. But she was and still is one of my best friends in the world. And now, I remember, still in shock, she is in love with me.

Once I heard Mike Nichols say something on a talk show. He said we live in decades. Some are good, some are bad. He said that is how he sees life. It made me think of Amber. Her decades have stood still. She is single. She is still a hippie. She is still my best friend. My decades had moved all over the place from the 40's to the 60's to the 70's to now. Up and down, sideways, and underneath. Her decades have gone in one horizontal direction, like a skyline over a 60's ocean. She has stayed true to her liberal politics, true to being a self-actualized woman. No one has moved her decades anywhere but right across that skyline of the 60's.

Haven

THE HYPNOTIST

Chapter 19

By: Haven

Dear Tempest:

Here is something that scared me. It was a movie called <u>Evidence</u> <u>of</u> <u>Love</u> starring Barbara Hersey. She plays a woman from a small town in Texas who kills her neighbor. But she isn't convicted of murder! She killed the woman with an axe. She has a tight little perm just like your psychic had. Tight and repressed. That was the attorney's argument: that she was repressed from her childhood and that she would never let her rage out so she had killed in self-defense. The movie made me cry. But it wasn't the murder. It was a scene when she was under hypnosis. The hypnotist got her to re-enact the murder and certain things from her childhood. She had not killed this lady in some pre-meditated fashion. She killed her to save herself. I understood. I could hear the truth in her voice. It was something about her voice. A voice can be so revealing.

    The hypnotist had me lie down on something like a massage table. He had a sexy, beautiful voice, an actor's voice, a bit like Richard Burton's. Soothing and strong. My father used to say Richard Burton had the most eloquent voice on the planet. Ever since then I have paid attention to voices more than most people do. Anyway, it was his voice. And, in this film, it was Barbara Hersey's voice.

I needed to find some answers. They were not only answers about Jerod. They were answers inside of me that I could be hiding in my subconscious. Did I want those to come out? I thought perhaps something could be revealed. You know, like in <u>The</u> <u>Sopranos</u> when the main guy starts revealing his inner child to Lorraine Bracco. She told him his depression is buried deep inside of him. Do you understand what I am saying? I knocked on the door and there was no answer. Not even a stirring. I knocked again. A silver haired man with an accordion wrapped around his torso answered. "Is it that time already? Haven?" I nodded. He stepped aside and I entered the cleanest, bluest room I had ever been in. Blue again. Must I be in a perpetually blue state? He saw my reaction. "Blue works best." He took off the accordion and motioned for me to sit down on the pretty blue sofa with blue pillows of different shades. The walls were a sky blue color. I closed my eyes a moment; I recall thinking that if I opened them, perhaps the entire color would change. Then, the way my mind does, I imagined the yellow of Nana and I suddenly wanted her there to make the room green. Her yellow combined with his blue would be a lovely green. Green, the color of Jerod's beautiful eyes. The hypnotist's voice jolts me from my daydreaming.

"Haven, are you okay?"

"Not so good," I blurted out. "My husband is missing. Did Amber tell you?" He nodded. He looked into my eyes and then did something strange. He reached out and stroked my hair. He smiled and whispered, "Baby fine." Then, "Lie down. Relax." So I did.

He told me to focus on the ceiling. I did. He began to tell me a beautiful story about an old couple that took walks by the sea everyday and cooked wonderful meals from food they grew in their garden; he described their farm, their lives, their children and before I knew it, I was asleep. All the while he stroked my hair. He told me to think of the room as my very own wailing wall, just like they have in Jerusalem. And like May has in <u>The Secret Life of Bees</u>. How I love that concept.

I want a wailing wall.

So, as far as being hypnotized—I cannot tell you much. Because I simply do not remember. But when I awoke I felt better. I felt clean and refreshed. And when I opened my eyes, I was alone in that blue room. He had left. There was soft music playing, two oatmeal cookies on a plate with milk like little kids leave for Santa on Christmas Eve, and tulips in a vase beside the cookies. Tulips. How did he know? I leaned over to smell them. I crunched into a cookie and drank the milk. There was a note on the table. "You know a lot more than you are letting on. Your secret about the money is safe with me. I think everything will be resolved. I found out you like tulips. And, there was a voice. It came out as a man's voice. He said, 'My spirit is so pained that it hurts just to be me.' I assume this was your husband speaking through you."

I gasped. Jerod had said those exact words to me. Now this accordian playing hypnotist knows some of my secrets! Obviously, my own crime was weighing heavily on my sub-conscious. Resolved? How? I decided to splurge and take a cab home. I leaned back and practiced deep breathing techniques. I got into the back of one on Broadway, right by the Strand, and I sat back. The driver turned around and looked at me a bit strangely when I gave him my address across town. Maybe I was being kidnapped now. I was starting to be mistrusting of everyone. He pulled out into traffic. It began to storm, the thunder crackled thick and loud. People dashed about with newspapers and briefcases over their heads. I looked up and at that moment I saw him. Jerod. At least I thought it was Jerod. He was being whisked along by a woman running up the street. Canan? They hopped into a green Land Rover and it sped off down Park Avenue. We turned at the corner of 57th and Park. A green SUV! Just like the one the lady in the Bronx had mentioned a wallet fell out of. Is Jerod here? But what about all my dreams? I dial my cell, calling Jack, as I whisk my head around looking back for them. There is nothing there. Had I imagined this?

"Stop! Stop!" I scream so loudly the driver jerks and stops, hitting the brakes mid stream. He bounces, I bounce and hit the top of my head on the ceiling of the back seat. The van too close behind us skids into a dramatic stop, spins around and almost hits another taxi like a scene from a movie. I reach up and my head is pounding. I have a bump. A big one. The cabdriver is angry. "Jesus, lady, you scared me. Now look at this mess."

I reach inside my purse, grab the 50 dollar bill I had been carrying, shove it at him and jump out looking around frantically. The driver gets out of the cab scratching his head and calls after me. "Where are you going?" I spot a N.Y. police car and run toward it. When I get there, I am drenched. The rain spatters on the face of my cell phone as I lift it to speak to Jack who is now on the other line. "I think I saw Jerod. But, now he's gone." De ja vu?

That night I dreamed about my father. I remembered things I hadn't thought about in ages. When someone dies, at first, all of these memories wash over you and fill you with sadness. For instance, once we slept in a tent in the back yard. My dad wasn't the camping sort, but this one time we did and my sisters and I all snuggled around him and listened to his ghost stories. One other time he took the morning off from work to bake cupcakes for my birthday and then he delivered them to my school. He was a "true blue" dad. The next day I promised the boys we would go camping in the upcoming summer months. We would sleep in tents and we would cook hot dogs and beans. If Jerod isn't coming back, I would need to be their true blue dad now.

Haven

CLUES, FINALLY!

Chapter 20

By: Haven

Dear Tempest:

I wanted to search Jerod's emails from our home computer but the police had taken it and still have it, of course. They finally gave me the content on a disc. Last night I started poring over them. Most are work related, a few were from him searching for travel deals, etc. One stuck out; it was an email he had saved. It was from Blake. He had written, "Come into my office, please. I want to discuss what happened last night. We need to clarify some things about this new client." I read it over and checked my calendar at home. That "last night" was a night of a parent teacher conference and Jerod was with me. He hadn't been to the office. Was Blake referring to my "Schintock" portfolio?

    I also recalled that Jerod said he needed Advil that night. He claimed he couldn't find any in the kitchen cabinet. He left for the store after we got home. He was gone for over an hour. Where was he? Once again I need to ask myself: had Jerod been blamed for my crime?

    Haven

HE WAS NOT INVINCIBLE

Chapter 21

By: Tempest

What Haven never knew and I found out later was exactly how deeply convoluted it was within the Tariks' business climate; Jerod's work took him into the secret financial underground. What Jerod had finally discovered, was that he was part of the Tariks' Ponzi scheme in ripping off clients to a huge degree. He had no idea that Haven's actions had made him look guilty of honing in on the scam. Usually, Blake acquired the clients. Sean created programs to keep the scheme looking authentic to clients and modified them masterfully with the changes in the economy so that folks still invested, believing naively that Tariks, Inc. was the only company still earning an 8-12% profit when most others were tanking around them. And Clint was the one who had thought up the scheme, researched other similar ploys, tracked successes and failures of specific eras and decades surrounding historical facets that made Ponzis work or not work. Mainly, Clint was willing to take the plunge, the risk. But it got so big that Schintock's portfolio escaped them. Each assumed the other was seeing it through not knowing none of them was doing so.

Jerod was unknowingly the front man. He was the one who kept the logs, talked to clients when they called, cashed out accounts when they insisted, did all of the superficial running of the business never knowing the truth lurking behind the phony fronts of varied spreadsheets. The brothers figured, if Jerod believed in the paperwork and "he works here", surely their clients would do the same. So, he served a few purposes; he processed lies and never knew it, and he served as the guinea pig for the brothers as they grew and expanded their plot to deceive more and more investors who were certain that Blake Tariks didn't have a dishonest bone in his body.

Everything was going along fine for a few years until the firm got so big they had to hire another front man; or, so they said. And they found the perfect person in Aihyan.. Blake, by now, was a billionaire; his brothers were as well, and Jerod had quite a nest egg growing he was hiding from Haven. The merit bonuses he was getting were his secret. It was his plan to surprise her with it along with a new house of her dreams, or if travels were what she preferred to the home, so be it. He still longed to make things up to her. He felt such remorse that it was like an opaqueness over his heart. And she never deserved that.

Aihyan was hired to work under Jerod; he had gone to Columbia and was at the top of his class. Young and clever, Jerod liked him and together they got the work done. It was obvious to me that he idolized Jerod. But it bothered me when the Tariks gave both of them the exact same bonus and gifts for Christmas. Money and cologne. I know Haven thought so and I, too, thought Jerod deserved more. After all, he had been there much longer. It's funny, though. This little bit of information, that Aihyan had gotten the same merit pay and cologne was a clue for me about Jerod. Jerod also found it odd and that is when he began to suspect Aihyan of having known the Tariks even before he was hired.

Jerod began to figure out that he was serving the purpose of dispersing fake information to clients while the Tarik brothers were taking from those that entrusted their savings to them and spending it on themselves. But he didn't know that his wife was milking them at their own game. When Jerod discovered what was happening, it cost him his freedom. This is how it happened the day Jerod figured out the truth: The phone rang. Jerod picked up, but before speaking, Blake had picked up the phone in his office at the same exact moment; Clint was on the other line. "Blake, I need you to transfer some of the Ottoman funds in right away. Escrow is closing and I need the funds." Jerod was ready to hang up the phone when Blake's reply stopped him dead cold. "Just have Jerod print up copies of the Silverstein investment sheets from last month and we can put new names on them. Hurry, I have a deadline."

"Will do. Give me a half an hour." Jerod waited for them both to hang up before he quietly replaced the receiver. He sat down feigning other work at his desk when Blake stepped out of his office and placed some forms in front of him. "Jerod, can you please copy these for me and tally the totals? The investor wants to see her profits right away." Jerod nodded, still numb at his discovery.

All of this information streamed to me in bits and pieces; yet, it was clear as day. Jerod was kidnapped off of the street corner near their apartment that very next day. The Tariks ordered it, Aihyan and Canan had manipulated it. Sophia, already in love with Jerod, was out of the loop. But her heart and her desire made her do her own searching for the man she had fallen so hard for.

How many secrets they were all keeping.

PONZI SCHEMES

Chapter 22

By: Haven

Dear Tempest:

I read more and more on the Internet all about Bernie Madoff and how he pulled off a Ponzi scheme. For years he blatantly lied to his investors claiming a constant profit, even in down times. People are so willing and anxious to trust someone with their money, it seems. I also discovered that in other countries, certain individuals have started attempting similar plots. Coincidentally, Turkey is one of them.

Things are starting to make more and more sense. On the way home I buy a DVD about Turkish culture. I learn all about the market places, the mosques, the people. I recognize things from my recurring nightmares. The room Jerod is in reminds me of alleys and buildings in Istanbul and I am more convinced than ever that he is hidden there. Then, I hear Bernie Madoff's son committed suicide. One journalist commented he must have known all about the Ponzi scheme and felt guilty. How would she know? Maybe he killed himself because he couldn't live with the guilt and pain from just having the same last name as his father. Sometimes, hurt wins out.

Haven

I GO BACK TO THE PSYCHIC

Chapter 23

DAY #14

By: Haven

Dear Tempest:

Amber feels I need to go back to Simone. I agree. I am lost without Jerod. It has been fourteen days now. I am falling into a deep depression. The cops have taken our house apart many times. I understand more, but also have more questions than answers; for example, where is the money Jerod supposedly hid? I want to go somewhere else, like where Marlon Brando escaped to. I want to hide in a cove of blue, as blue as Amber's eyes.

    Today, Simone is wearing oranges and purples with lots of beads around her neck and round John Lennon like sunglasses. She swings the door wide open when I arrive. "Come in. Your nana's humming is making me crazy."

    I step into her familiar living room. I sit on the same sofa I had sat on before, with Amber. She sits beside me and takes my hands in hers. "Oh, shush up already!" She snaps at the little puff of yellow energy in the space of air between us. Humming rushes at me in bursts. "Nana," I lean into the yellow that looks like a puff of cotton candy. "Nana, help me. Jerod has been gone for two weeks and I need your help."

Instantly, the yellow spreads around me and I feel arms hugging me.

Nana's voice comes softly, "He is alive."

Simone falls onto the rug. It is a real Persian of all colors muted and stitched together; the oranges and purples of her gown blend with the rug. She doesn't move. I look down at her. Her face is pale. This is so much like your psychic when Dolphin Dad appeared that first time. These poor mediums. What a job. I get up and tip toe to the kitchen to wet a paper towel. I return to Simone and dab her forehead with it. Her eyelids flutter. "He is still alive. You have to find him, Haven. He loves you so much."

She pulls a knitted blanket down from the top of the sofa and wraps herself inside of it staying on the floor curled up blending with her carpet. "Please go. Leave the money on the table by the door. It is more now. Two hundred dollars." I do as I am told and place the cash on the table. Geez. Her price has gone up!

Jerod is still alive! Was my vision on the streets of Manhattan all in my head?

Haven

RANDOM HEARTS

Chapter 24

By: Haven

Dear Tempest:

I finally watch this movie you recommended. The main male actor is Harrison Ford and his wife dies in a car accident. He discovers she was unfaithful only after she has died. Then, Kristen Scott Thomas, the wife of the lover of Harrison's dead wife, finds out the same about her husband. Individually, and separately, they are devastated when their respective spouses die together in a plane crash after having had an affair *with each other.*

    Then I have a marathon. I have never been so depressed. I watch <u>Unfaithful</u> again. I watch <u>The Women</u>. I watch <u>How to Make an American Quilt</u>. I watch <u>Taken</u> and <u>Ransom</u> and so on. Anything I can find about kidnapping and infidelity, I watch. I cry and cry. I use an entire box of Kleenex and feel completely and utterly numb. My leave from the hospital will end in two weeks, but I am worried I can never get the strength to go back to work. I wonder if the kids would be better off without me.

    Nana always said things look better in the morning and she was right. Jack came over the next day and we take a drive and look everywhere for that damn car. I know Tempest has sent him. We drive down every street, all over Manhattan. The green

Land Rover is nowhere. The cops think I am nuts because they called me to inform me they had found another car with someone who resembled Jerod. I still think it is just too close to be a coincidence. Jack has traced Sophia's parents to Little Italy and has questioned them. She is traveling throughout Europe, they think. So, I breathe relief that she is far, far away. Jack also did a handwriting analysis on Aihyan's letter; he matched things from the office: Aihyan did write the note to me. Now, the cops have begun to trace his cell calls and think he is in Istanbul. The Tariks are in jail; they have confessed to money laundering and embezzlement. They claim they know nothing about Jerod's whereabouts. Jack also talked to Sophia's landlady. There is one thing. Sophia had casually mentioned to her landlady that she was interested in traveling to Turkey. And, there was a brochure about coming attractions in Istanbul left in her trash can. So, she could be in Turkey. Also, Jack found a key sewn into the corner of Jerod's wallet. The cops missed it and so did I. We traced it to a P.O. box in the Upper West and the box contained those items Jerod had previously pawned and gotten back. Now, what was this all about? It is all so confusing and so disturbing. Did he need cash and then was able to buy the objects back again?

    Haven

THE PARKING TICKETS SHE GOT

Chapter 25

By: Tempest,
Do you remember the scenes on the train with Diane Lane in Unfaithful*? Do you remember her expression after the first time she made love with the young Italian guy? I do. Vividly. It was mixture of guilt and joy. Guilt and joy. I hate to admit this—but Haven needs to recognize that anyone involved in a satisfying affair has that same expression on his or her face. I wonder, did Jerod wear that face? And do you recall all the parking tickets she got while parked in the Village while she was visiting her lover? I do. She could have cared less about the tickets. That is what wild, obsessed sex does to you. You care less about practical matters and want another fix—that caress, that moment of ecstasy. I get it. After Jerod disappeared, Haven had found some tickets hidden in that damn closet again. But, they were new tickets, not old ones from a year ago. I wonder, were there tickets from meeting up with Canan? Or, were they from seeing Sophia again? I only had a rumor by one of the boys that he and Canan had "flirted." I had Haven's emotional and physical assault on her. I had the fact that Haven thinks Canan searched her wallet once. I had that Canan is striking looking. The*

neighbors Jack went to question had nothing negative to say about her; yet, when asked about Jerod and her together, they were strangely quiet. Something is still out of sync and I do not know what it is. I wish my psychic powers would kick in. Mario ended up staying here to assist with Sarah and Molly so we had to let Haven down. Jack has stepped in and is there helping her but Haven needs her husband to come home.

Jack always says look for the obvious in the unobvious places.

Or did he say look for the unobvious in the obvious places?

I AM BARELY HANGING ON

Chapter 26

DAY #15

By: Haven

Dear Tempest:

It has been more than two weeks now. I considered taking my own life but what would the boys do? It is just this isn't the life I had worked so hard for. I need to take it a day at a time like they say in AA and NA. But, I hate waking up from this bad dream every morning. I am worried about Justin. He picked a fight at school yesterday. It is because he misses his dad. His teacher says he is tense, not concentrating. He is my one who is not school material to begin with, so this is difficult. I decide to let him stay home with me today and we rent a DVD, make delicious sandwiches and do a jigsaw puzzle. It's necessary to spend time with just one of your children at a time sometimes. Jeremy is older, he is fighting harder to seem cool right now; so, the only time Justin gets to still be a boy, without trying to look tough, is when Jeremy is gone. We go on a hike at the park, get breakfast and then decide to watch October Sky, because Jerod had watched it once before with him. Jerod was with us in spirit the whole time.

    Jack is fully on the case now and has discovered more and more information about Aihyan. Jack says our answer is with Aihyan in Istanbul. Now the cops have traced him on a first class flight there. I decide it is worth the money to send Jack there. So, he comes over for a final discussion with me about all we know and we start to make arrangements.

Then, something jumps out at me like what happened to Paul Newman in <u>The Verdict</u>. I recall this movie is one of Tempest's favorites. Now I know why. It is so feasible that someone can be bribed to seduce a man like Jerod. That is a part in this film. All of the facts run together in my head now. Sophia wants more than Jerod. Does she want my life much the same way Creepo wanted Tempest's? Sophia supposedly wanted to visit Turkey. Is that where she is? I stabbed Canan. She didn't press charges. Why not? Jerod had researched the background of the Tariks and put our money somewhere; it is not in our regular accounts. Where is it? Was that to protect us or to save himself? He pawned things then bought them back. Why? The cops uncovered enough information to help get the Tariks arrested. But is it enough to be sure they would be indicted? Then, they kept me out of the loop, why? My stomach is a mess. I have developed acid reflex but it isn't from being fifty something. It is from stress. And, the cops haven't found Jerod or Aihyan yet. Nor, have they learned about my embezzlement. Or, have they? The Tariks have been their priority. Jack and I have figured out a lot. Yet, not what matters most.

Upstairs, on the roof deck that I hardly ever visit, we have a wicker sofa and a wicker chair. They are white and weather beaten, but the cushions stand up to the weather. It is a rare warmish day, and I am still pondering what I do know and don't know when I decide to go up there. Just last week we had a blizzard and an old man down the street had died from not putting on his heater. But today, the sun is warming the city of New York. So, I head up to the deck. Under the warming sun while sitting on the chair, looking out over the Chelsea market and craving some fresh coffee, I notice a bump below me, under the cushion.

I stand and lift it!

A ziplock bag full of small yellow sheets of paper stare back at me. I hurry grabbing the bag. I cannot believe it. This could be the moment I have been waiting for. Nana is now sitting on a wall opposite me. The humming is calm for a change, comforting. It is to an old classic, "Once in a While." I open the bag and begin reading.

Jerod had compiled all the evidence he needed to bring the Tariks to the authorities for millions of dollars they had stolen from clients. Millions and millions. Twenty-eight to be exact. The amount I stole isn't mentioned. He had written it out longhand with a letter to me. Names, dates, amounts. He trusted no one but me, he said. He also said if he was gone, they took him. He would be either dead or somewhere being held because of the information he had discovered. I read over these small yellow pad papers again and again. Wait until he finds out about my scam! I had sent my money to Puerto Rico to hide. But now... what to do with all of this information?

Haven

TURKEY

Chapter 27

By: Haven

Dear Tempest:

I called the authorities and was suddenly surrounded by cops and securities officials for hours. They left with the papers. I woke up last night remembering that photo among the cards I had found. The one of *her* when she was standing on a balcony and behind her head were those wind chimes; the ones with silver tubes with fish on them. But something else I hadn't noticed before. Way far away, in a shadow inside the door is Aihyan. In the middle of the night, with a full moon in the sky, I stare at those damn wind chimes for twenty minutes before more came to me.

That windchime had been hanging on Canan's balcony. And the scene of the skyline off of the balcony was Canan's view. I am reminded that Canan could always watch when Jerod and the boys walked up the street to the subway. But mostly, it was the proof I needed of the Sophia/Canan/Aihyan connection.

The next morning I make a color copy of the photo and take it to the detectives. It ties Sophia not only to Canan, but now to Aihyan. But would it do anything to help find Jerod? Meanwhile, things are going on in Turkey. I have no idea what, but I keep visualizing Istanbul temples and streets; they are places I have seen in movies or books. And I have this vision:

Aihyan looked over at the Taksim Square this early evening one last time to see if she was coming. He scanned the air, looking for her auburn flocked head. The unusual color always made her stand out, as did her clothes she wore. Colorful and bright. But, Canan was nowhere to be seen. Then Aihyan decided to pay for tea and join the crowds flowing into the Istiklal Caddesi. It was Saturday night and it was hard to move without hitting people every now and then. He heard joyful laughs of young people socializing. A gypsy was selling flowers, yellow tulips. He remembered that Jerod's wife loved tulips. That was a small piece of the information he had had to memorize about Jerod's family. Poor woman. He felt sorry for her now, but the money the Tariks had paid him to get rid of his co-worker was worth it. Plus, they were in prison now anyway, since some evidence surfaced. It seemed like for a long, long time. Aihyan had wondered how the cops got the information and so specific at that. Only Jerod could have leaked it. The problem was now he wasn't getting anything out of the son of a bitch. And, even worse, he liked the guy. He wasn't a murderer; damn it. Jerod was so closed mouthed Aihyan was surprised. He even admired him. Why should he kill him now? The brothers were locked away. Couldn't he just let the poor sucker go? Mazhar Alanson's lyrics: "I have bought yellow tulips to you from Çiçek Pazarı," rang out by a random young musician with his guitar case open for coins. Sokak was always the perfect place for anyone to drink raki and eat fish. He would buy some for him and Canan. She loved fish. But, he did not enter Nevizade; instead, he walked a few minutes more, then stopped in front of the old apartment, more than hundreds of years old, with high ceilings. He gazed at the black metal door, opened it with his key, pushed hard on it and entered the outside living area that housed the dark, hidden room where Jerod was being held. There was a frowzy smell in the air; he stepped into the darkness where a slight light from the new moon cast its face upon Jerod, tied to a chair, tape across his mouth, with bloodied, bruised legs stretched out in front of him. Aihyan's cell phone lit up and the odd bell ringing tune startled the tortured American as he raised his head wearily to the sound.

Aihyan wondered how much longer he should wait before killing the American. The Tariks had kept their part of the bargain in paying him, and he had strict instructions for when to kill Jerod, yet surely, wouldn't a kidnapping alone be helpful to their plight?

Opera was the favorite form of theatre in 19th century Istanbul. A troupe from Italy performed for an entire season at one theatre, while French operas were staged at another. Istanbul was one of a handful of opera capitals in Europe. Sophia just loved opera and it was another reason she came here. Canan had filled her in about the opera scene in Istanbul. She took in all the smells of the market place when Aihyan briskly walked past her and a cologne he was wearing made its way to her. He smelled like Jerod. She had to admit, she had almost lost her mind by falling in love with Jerod. She was insanely jealous of his wife and went far above the call of duty when she blackmailed him in the end. And, now, here she was, because Canan had told her all about the beautiful, country called Turkey and how Istanbul was a city of wonderful culture. She knew they might bring him here. She knew of the millions the Tariks had hidden, she knew their capability for international escapades. Canan had told her the stories. So, Sophia did what no one else had done; she had come here to find Jerod. But she also knew Canan and Aihyan had been paid handsomely to cover up the money laundering, the hiring of certain individuals (including herself). She had some information to go on. She hadn't gotten closer to Canan than she had to for nothing. That day she went to her apartment, when Canan left to use the bathroom, Sophia had uncovered an Istanbul address. How easy it had been. Then, she hoped, if she was the one to free Jerod, surely he would come back to her.

She stood in the square listening to the young tour guide speaking in English with a Turkish lilt, "It was June 1934. The Shah of Iran was going to visit Turkey from the 10th of June to the 6th of July." She stopped. That's when that same men's cologne aroma hit her again, she turned to follow Aihyan, a crumpled piece of paper in her hand. She lowered the brim of her red hat and followed Aihyan. And that was it. My vision was so real I could taste it. I reached for the phone to call Jack.

    Haven

A DREAM

Chapter 28

By: Haven

Dear Tempest:

Jack is on his way flying to Istanbul. I do not know if he will make it in time. After that vision, my mind is working over time and this is the dream I had tonight; it is the worst ever.

MY DREAM:

Jerod is sitting in a room, a dark room. His hands are shackled to the posts of the bed. His feet are shackled as well. He is thin and purple and blue from being beaten. Dried blood covers parts of his body and his nose has been broken. Canan comes in and pours water into his mouth and he almost drowns in it choking because she can't stop for him to take a breath. Her hair is as it has always been, spiked, auburn, short. She is in great shape, a natural gymnist looking type. Suddenly Aihyan comes in and places his hands around Jerod's throat choking him. I can only see him from the back. He says, "I have been ordered to kill you."

At this point, I wake up perspiring. Why are they wanting him dead? Did Jerod take money, too? Is it hiding somewhere? Did I compound Jerod's problems by stealing money from the Tariks in my insane moments of jealousy and anger? I wonder; your dreams were so close to real life. Are mine? I shiver and it is not even cold. I get up and make coffee.

I call and arrange for a ninety minute massage. I know. It is selfish. It is so decadent. I need it. I want to cry it out—all of it. The guilt. The worry. The pain.

I arrive at Claudia's and she is ready for me. She works from home. She is a short, fit Mexican woman who loves doing yoga in a steam room. She has lavender in vases around the room, and lovely seashore sounds are being piped in from the stereo somewhere in her apartment. A soon as I arrive, I see the candles, smell the lavender. As I take off my backpack, something falls to the floor. An old cell phone of Jerod's! It is one I had forgotten all about; one he kept active but hardly used. We didn't cancel it because it was on a contract and we were waiting for it to run out. How could I have forgotten about it? I shove it back into the bottom pocket but now I am completely consumed by wanting to check the calls on it. How could I possibly relax now? But, I have come here, made an expensive appointment, and I have to wait.

Back to Claudia's table. I undress and slip onto the table under the Egyptian cotton sheets. Blue. Blue everywhere, I swear. These people like the hypnotist and Claudia must know I am blue. I lie down on my stomach despite my new discovery; before I know it I am asleep. I must be lying there ten minutes before I hear her steps. "I decided to just let you alone for a bit. You needed the quiet." She is one of the sweetest ladies. She runs way over the time she is paid for. She goes the extra mile with hot rocks, warm wash cloths, etc. I am literally in heaven on earth on Claudia's massage table.

I start off okay. But then I begin to cry. The deeper she rubs, the more I weep. She says it is like I was weeping for my entire life. She asks why. I tell her:

It is because everyone in my life goes missing. My mom, the same as missing. My Nana, dead. My father, dead. Tony, missing for years. Now, Jerod, missing from my world.

Haven

OSCAR AWARDS NIGHT and THE CELL PHONE

Chapter 29

By: Haven

Dear Tempest:

Still, after Claudia, I feel better. I come home and have a green tea with ice and I feel better. I pull out the dinosaur phone of Jerod's seeing it needs to be charged. I go to the drawer where I keep old plugs and wires and chords. After a lot of tries, I find the right charger and plug it in. Now I have to wait. An hour passes, I unplug the phone and turn it on. No recent calls. No dialed calls. But there are two text messages saved.

From her.

The first says, "if you do not leave her I will kill myself." The second reads, "when you go home and make love to her it is like you are stabbing me in my heart." Talk about melodramatic. Jerod had saved these two messages. Why? Proof of her involvement or because he liked reading about her lusty obsession with him? No matter. I am getting rid of this phone. Who needs this? This is one piece of evidence no one needs to know about. I turn on the gas fireplace and throw it into the flames. A strange odor escapes into the air: the odor of "them" and how intense it was. I crawl into a ball on our pillow chair and watch her texts go up in red and yellow oblivion.

Will I survive this?

My mind wanders. *It has to.*

I think how it is that time of year. Awards time for those of us addicted to movies. Me, you, your friends, my friends. I decide that I am spending so much time just waiting for news, waiting for something, I need to do something. I know we are almost there—finding out where he is, if he is dead or alive and if I don't do something to occupy myself and the boys, I will go crazy.

Jeremy is separating in a way. He is on the phone a lot. He leaves and meets friends in different parts of the city. How I wish Jerod were here to help compromise with him on all these things he now thinks he is old enough for. I know he is just doing what I am doing. He is escaping this hell we are living through.

Everything is just different now. I have no idea where or how my life will proceed. Will I be a widow? That is when I reread your account of her Oscar party and I decide to just do one. There is no news from the detectives and the boys need a diversion. It is so last minute but still I call both Amber and Cynthia and ask them to invite friends over to my house. Justin, so sweet, says he will cook some hot dogs and hamburgers for us, and I decide that this year I will be Penelope Cruz. I am taller, and I am bigger. But I am dark, and I have a pretty face. Like you, I do not go to a thrift store. Instead I go online and spend hours checking out past photos of her at Oscar, Golden Globe and SAG parties. There is one black dress that sort of fans out at her feet, like a mermaid. I love it.

I call every consignment shop in New York City until finally a woman tells me she might have something I would like. I am embarrassed to tell her I am a size 10. I am a completely normal, beautiful size. But this stupid, stupid society has made me feel like sh—because I am a 10. Go figure.

Amber comes as Sigourney Weaver. It sort of hurts my feelings when she tells me it's a stretch, my being Penelope Cruz. I laugh but inside I am a little stung. I think the opposite about her. I think she is more gorgeous than Sigourney. Oh well. We eat cheese and gourmet crackers, have the burgers and hot dogs, drink some wine and watch the awards. It is fun, but I start to cry for no reason and, of course, it is because I miss Jerod and I am waiting to hear from Jack. I try to forget about everything tonight but it doesn't work. I am feeling like I can find out any minute that he is gone forever. I had told myself so many times, if it goes over fourteen days, he will be dead. I sit here with this gorgeous black mermaid dress on that looks like the one Penelope wore. I am beautiful, but my life is an ugly mess.

In the middle of the show there is a special "BREAKING NEWS" interruption. It is an announcement about a man who has been found in Korea. He has been living in South Korea for over thirty-three years. I lean in to the television and I can see Tony. He is middle aged now with deep lines in his forehead and beside his eyes.

But it is him.

The newscaster is explaining how he was missing in action in the Vietnam War. He says Mr. Milano will not comment right now and is taking a special plane to Germany first for examinations by the proper parties in the military. It is questionable about why he is in Korea now.

Next, his mother is on the screen and her eyes are more alive than I have ever seen them. She is crying with joy. Beside her is Maria, Tony's wife, also over fifty, still the young pretty woman Tony had chosen to marry. She is crying, too. You see, I had made up this dream for all these years that Tony and I still loved one another. But the Tony I dreamed of was the Tony from thirty years ago. This man has lived a thousand other lives since I knew him long ago.

Haven

THANK GOD ONE OF US KNOWS WHAT'S GOING ON

Chapter 30

By: Tempest

The detective in Istanbul had gotten several leads from an old vegetable stand vendor who walked past Jerod's hidden room almost daily. At first she saw a single light in the room that used to be dark at all times and found it odd. Then, she made a point of walking past to see if it was always on. Now, today, she reported to the police that there was a stunning young Italian woman wearing a floppy red hat who was watching the old style apartment unit, too.

That same day she carried a foot-stool, bigger than that kitchen type, but smaller than a painter's ladder. It was quite early, earlier than most of the vendors would even open their shops. And just like that, at the end of Jerod's 16th day of being held here, beaten and starving, hands tied to a dirty bed, a rat making its way across the cement floor, the old woman hoisted herself up the ladder and peeked into the window and saw him. A young girl, five or so, had appeared to her in her bedroom and she had beckoned Naciye to follow her. She was a beautiful child, the apparition I call Caroline. It wasn't the first one Naciye had seen. Old people see them sometimes, you see. They just do not mention it. So, that day, Naciye followed the small ghost and after climbing up and peering through the window, when she saw Jerod, calmly, she climbed down. She went to the open-air market where potatoes and cucumbers and zucchini lined the carts, and told her young assistant she would be back much later. She and Caroline stood side by side and watched then as the tall man named Aihyan and his wife Canan left by taxi from the square. But, these two were no longer what mattered to her; she wanted to help the American and the further away they were, the better. She climbed into the public transit bus and went directly to police headquarters where she demanded to see the head detective. She told him her story. He had gotten yet another bulletin from the NYPD, sending out a warrant for searching for a Turkish man named Aihyan Cleyet, who had disappeared in Chelsea 16 days prior and was believed to be in Istanbul. And now this chubby private detective was standing before him with photos and ideas. But, it was this woman's sighting that was the break he had been waiting for. He went to the fax machine retrieving photos once again of Jerod Rodriquez and the couple known as Aihyan and Canan. Then he sent the photos over his

Blackberry to every police officer on duty in Istanbul.

When the police and Jack rushed the alley and broke down the door, Jerod was delirious. Canan and Aihyan were long gone; they had finally decided to spare his life. He was, in excruciating pain, but alive. They had left him to die. If it hadn't been for the elderly, astute woman who found him, he would have. Just about the same instant, Sophia hurried toward the alley with a policeman on her heels. As she arrived, shadowed under the brim of her hat, she gasped at seeing the man she loved in such horrible condition. She rushed to him.

She leaned over to whisper in his ear. "I will never leave you." He did not fully understand what she was there for, as Haven and his sons were the only ones who existed for him. She was nothing but a horrible mistake from his past and he prayed for her to simply disappear. "Go away, Sophia. I never want to see you again," he could barely mumble. She took in the air around her as if it and Jerod's cruel words stung her; and as she glanced around at all the spectators, she pulled the red hat down low, backing into the crowd.

SOME THINGS HAVE BEEN RESOLVED

Chapter 31

DAY #18

By: Haven

Dear Tempest:

I still do not understand a lot of it. The cops simply haven't found Aihyan or Canan. Sophia has fessed up to her part; but, after all, she is only guilty of adultery and accepting a bribe. I still haven't told Jerod a word about the money I stole. I have so much guilt that they may have kidnapped him thinking he stole it. Some secrets need to stay secrets until the right time for coming out of hiding.

    Sophia won't even get jail time. She admitted Canan was the person who hired her to seduce Jerod last year. Despite being captured, drugged and beaten, Jerod lived. The Tariks were all over the news again last night about their upcoming trials and Jerod's being found. Apparently there are two famous actresses who got taken in by them and a lot of older New York residents that lost a lot of money. Once Jerod regains some strength, he will have depositions to deal with. No matter that he didn't know about the extent of their schemes nor that he didn't do anything illegal himself; he still will have to prove that.

    Do you remember the money he borrowed, the refinancing I was so concerned about? The broach he sold? Jerod was a step ahead. As soon as he became suspicious, he had done that so things would appear as if we had heavy debt so there was no way we could show profits and unusual deposits. Jerod was smarter than I had given him credit for. Meanwhile, he had put the cash bonuses in a safe place.

Haven

JEROD IS HOME!

Chapter 32

By: Haven

Dear Tempest:

Jerod has been home for three days.

The memories of everything we have been through still hits me in waves. I try the fog and rain thing where I put fog over many of my memories. I should just be content. He is alive. The boys seem amazingly back to normal and have been tender and loving with their father. Jeremy, the quintessential young teen in some ways while acting thirty in others, is home more and it feels like he has crawled back into his real skin. Jerod's mom and sister have been very sweet and understanding of our need to be alone. And, even though it seems now like it happened a zillion years ago, before Canan, before the kidnapping, before the Tariks hired Aihyan, before my arrest, before Simone and hypnotist--the infidelity still hurts. I will never quite understand how he succumbed to Sophia, weakened. I stand in the kitchen making coffee to bring to him, just the way he likes it, and I wonder, deep, deep down in my Aries soul, will I ever get over this entire experience and be able to go on with my own life, my own dreams? Will I always be envisioning her in a black sultry negligee and will that thong ever leave my mind? Will the pain of wondering if Jerod may have never truly loved me ever completely disappear? And, I know that the answer is two folded.

No and Yes. You see, the haunting scenes will diminish with time. But never completely. And as far as his loving me? He is here, isn't he? He never left us. He ordered tulips for me yesterday. All colors of the rainbow. Maybe that is the real rainbow I am supposed to follow. Besides, what matters is what I can live with. We all make mistakes.

Dear Tempest, you killed because you knew you had to. I stabbed because I was out of control. You grieved the death of Peter. But I have Jerod back and we have a second chance.

Jerod has a lot of pain from what he let happen. As do I. I hear humming and see Nana outside the window and I think of Katie. Unable to ever walk. And Caroline, the little watchful soul. I think of Jack, I smile at the thought of Simone, the odd blue loving hypnotist, everyone who helped me. Justin has just painted a still life of the tulips Jerod gave to me yesterday and it is stunning. When I see the boys , relief and elation in their faces, I know I will do my best to erase the memories of things I need to erase. I look outside again and there is Nana, spinning gently near her hummingbird feeder with her misty yellow cloud around her. She reminds me of a lemon colored snow cone that my father used to buy for me when I was a kid in Yonkers. Cotton candy and snow cones, not a bad way to go!

Haven

SOPHIA COMES TO VISIT

Chapter 33

By: Haven

Dear Tempest:

Am I asleep or awake? Am I dreaming? Oh God. Do not let me forget this dream.

ANOTHER DREAM:

There is a knock at the door. I will never know how she got into the building. But then, her husband had managed to do the same thing a week ago. I had just colored my hair by myself, with highlights. You can buy the package that way now. My hair still has a lot of dark brown in it and now that Jerod is home, I have been trying to do some things to feel better. Younger. Prettier. Highlights on our lives. We need it. We have said to one another it is time we take better care of each other. I had just looked into trips to Ireland, Brazil, Italy, and Malta. These are places we have always wanted to go. Like you, Tempest. You wanted to travel with Peter more. *You never got to.*

Jerod wants to look into his ancestors who traveled from Italy to Puerto Rico. There goes that Italian thing again. Also, my uncle in Puerto Rico has written to us that he has a vacation house on the water he is willing to let us use with the boys, come August. I have plans of telling Jerod about the money when we go there. Yes, it is still my secret and the money is still there. But here she is, standing here, at my door, gorgeously petite and Italian as ever. Both hands are concealed in the pockets of the peach colored blazer she has on. The blazer matches a floral print skirt that falls deliciously down around her calves. She is wearing new red sandals, feminine ones I imagine she bought to match that red hat I have heard about. Her toenails match her blazer. Every little thing has been attended to with detail. Her lips are lush and melon colored. Melon, like the color Nana and I always wore when I was a kid. My heart swells with resentment that she is wearing shades of melon.

"Hello, Sophia."

"Haven. We finally meet."

A voice called out from the den. "Mom, I'm hungry!" Justin is always starving as soon as he wakes up. You and I had laughed about this once. You mentioned both your boys were like that when they were growing up.

Sophia Gemignani lifts her hand out of one of the pockets from the blazer and in it is a small silver gun. She aims it right at my stomach. But then she points it up a bit, more toward my heart. I realize, at that moment: she is planning to shoot me in my heart! "You have already broken my heart, Sophia. You do not need to shoot it, too," I whisper to her. "I am sorry Haven. I still love him." She licks her melon lips, clicks the gun to taunt me.

I finally understood why my name is missing that damn "e." I will not know heaven, true heaven, until I get rid of her. It is right at that same moment, all in a split second, I hear footsteps to my side, behind the foyer stucco wall; I sense him. "Mom!" Justin calls out again, hungry, from the den as he watches a commercial. Jerod reaches out from behind the wall and pushes me as hard as he can against the opposite archway; I fly as if I am a feather. He lunges at her.

A shot goes off.

Then another. They both lie there. My head hurts so much where it has hit the wall; it feels like a crowbar has smacked it. I look up and see Jeremy staring down at his father. Then, more footsteps, and Justin is looking down at them, then at me, with eyes popping out of his head. The shock wears off just enough for him to speak: "Mom. Daddy's hurt. He's bleeding." As I creep over to Jerod, there is yellow surrounding him. Nana's here. Calmly, Jeremy whispers: "Mommy, Daddy protected you like I told you he would." I nod. I close my eyes and I can see them all: Dolphin Dad, Nana, and Jerod. Jerod, a ghost, is smiling down at me and he reaches out to brush the hair out of my eyes. "I'm sorry, Haven. I never meant to hurt you. I will always love you."

Haven

ONE MONTH LATER

Chapter 34

By: Haven

Dear Tempest,

I know it has been a while. I got your message. I also saw your blog entry recently about your daughter's film, the addition you are planning for your home, and, congratulations on your engagement to Mario! I am sorry I didn't call you right back. I have Jerod home, and we have been so busy. You can imagine. I have so much to tell you. Tempest, now that he is home, I am going to try, henceforth, not to speak of this horrible event. Even with Jerod. If he mentions any of it, it simply never happened. It is just too upsetting. Meanwhile, you know all the details. You must, absolutely must, delete the description of my final dreams after reading. I have heard we release anger into the air with our dreams. I am hopeful this last dream I am sharing will release my anger into the air forever.

Tempest, thank you for everything. I hope Sarah is healing. We are all right now. I have to move on, and learn to forgive and forget. Last night, after we were all asleep I awoke. Jerod wasn't in bed and I jumped up. I rushed into the living room; he was sitting on the couch looking out the window. He had our wedding album on his lap. I sat beside him and together we turned the pages in silence, the moon's light casting its light on that day that bonded us so long ago. The same moon that shed its light on him in that horrible room in Istanbul. Then we went back to sleep and this is:

MY FINAL DREAM:

I am planning Sophia's murder. I have been doing this for days. Months. I am tired of picturing her. I am tired of trying to forgive her. I am tired of her lips, her negligee. She did wrong. And I am so tired of visual imagery. It doesn't work like the real thing. Secretly, I have the feeling Joseph wants her dead, too. There is life insurance, after all. He deserves it. He whispered something to me before he left that day. He whispered, "This is all her fault, Haven. She did it. Jerod was a pawn in their game. Don't blame him. Blame her." But it was what he said next that stuck with me. "It is okay, Haven. Whatever you need to do. It is okay." Did he mean what I thought he meant? Was he giving me permission to murder his wife?

Indeed.

I push her off of a ferry on the Hudson as it encircles The Statue of Liberty. I decide the Pacific Northwest is too far away. But right here, in the river, sharks rush to devour her, piece by piece. (Yes, I know there are no sharks in the river, but this is a dream…) Blood rushes to the surface of the gray water. Gray and red make an ugly charcoal colored purple. Then, I move ahead to my next imagery dream sequence. I am on top of the Empire State Building on the last tour for tourists. I glance over mischieviously at her as she looks out over the city. I smile at her, disguised in my Marilyn platinum wig and large sunglasses. I could be Marilyn. She does a double take trying to determine who I am under the blonde hair. I move close to her and even though tourists are all around, I take her wrist and turn it back, twisting it hard, spitting these words at her, "Guess what? You are about to jump." I yank and pull and finally get her to a place where she climbs above the off limits wire railing; it is her final moment. And she obeys me. She knows if she doesn't jump she will be pushed. She flies off into her own personal abyss, to the ground far below. I rush over, she looks like a dragon fly as she heads down, arms stretched out to her side. A green dragon fly. She bounces off of a taxi cab and flies into the street. Her death is far too painless.

But neither of those is feasible. I go into the kitchen. It is still very early. The guys are sleeping. I look up that language school once more. The Linghe School. I write down the address for the zillionth time. I take a shower. I look good. All this hell has made me lose ten pounds. I have done this run umpteen times rehearsing. It has burned off two sizes. I dress in my size 8 sweats and a hooded sweatshirt that says "The Highline" on it. I grab my Teva tennis shoes that always need double knots and I go to Jerod who is still half asleep in bed, lying on his side in his blue snowflake pajamas. I whisper into his ear a lie of huge proportions, one he will never hear the truth of. "I am going for a walk to the market. I'll get bagels. Be back in a while." He nods dreamily, turning the other way into his pillow.

Safe and sound.

I walk silently, in my killer tennis shoes, through the dining room. I reach for a small but sharp knife (the one we use to slice bagels) out of the way back of our silverware drawer. It has been planted there for a month. It has been sharpened beyond sweet in its shine and blade proficiency. It is a point of perfection. It glistens with reflections of me as I stare into it, my face, my eyes, my insanity edged with just enough clarity stares back at me in the silver reflection. I am beautiful. Damn I look good a size 8. As pretty as she is. Prettier, I decide. That fine line between being sane and insane you understand in women like me (only too well) is there.

In my eyes.

I start in long graceful strides toward north Chelsea, my hand clasped around the knife that is wrapped in a thick plastic bag in my pocket, careful not to touch the blade. I cut over, heading toward Mid Town. It will take a good twenty blocks to get to the school. The schedule said 9 a.m. for her first class. She just resumed work. The cops were more than willing to let her get back to her class as long as she sticks around for questioning. Eventually, it will all come out. Her affair with Jerod. Her following him to Turkey. Her being paid to seduce him. Maybe even more I do not know about.

Her last class.

I need to arrive shortly before her, take her by surprise. Hunkered down in my hood with my new highlights, I take deep cleansing breaths to oxygenate my soul in bravado. I get there before the ugly, short Mafia looking owner even unlocks the door. It's exactly 5 minutes to 9. Perfect. First, he pushes up the iron gate. Then, the keys jostle as he struggles with the lock. I am close by, pretending to tie my shoes. He has not seen me, my highlights or my Highline sweatshirt. He has not seen the secrets in my Aries eyes or the pain of my Aries soul. He has no idea. He goes in to start a day with only money on his stupid, petty little mind.

Here she comes. Wearing a cute plaid skirt with a white button up collar blouse, all cotton. The blouse has a Peter Pan collar. And she has on Converse tennis shoes. Does she think she is fooling anyone with this high school innocence look? This mask she wears over her devilish persona? This horrible woman who didn't care one bit that she could have ruined our family we had worked so hard to nourish and grow. I step back, barely, into a tiny alley beside the front gate. It had just enough shadow there. I could do this thing to her and leave her. We can spend some real quality time together. No one would see me. Or her. I look up squinting; yes, the weak sun is in the right place in the sky. I know I will be questioned soon. I am the wife. I was the emotionally distraught spouse. And two million was still missing. But, I had won over the detectives on our case. One by one. I had done what needed to be done. An espresso here, a gelato ice here, a piece of coconut cream pie even. The detectives love me now. They are my "guys." They would never suspect me. Never. I had kept that as another little

Aries secret from you, dear reader and you, too dear Tempest. I had won over the policemen and Jack. No one would even suspect what I had planned for sick Hour glass Sophia.

"Excuse me, pardon me." She stops, her eyes sparkling with arrogance. Sicilian. I see them up close now. Her eyes are way more southern than Italian. I bet she is Sicilian. "Yes?" She even has the Italian accent. "Pardon me, can you help me a moment? I need to find…" I pretend that I need her help with directions. I stick a piece of paper out for her to see. It is one of her letters she wrote to Jerod. She leans in. Her eyes widen. Just enough. I yank her closer. She is too dismayed, too confident to believe something or someone can take her by surprise.

I can do this. The little housewife from Chelesa. The not so desperate New York housewife this time. "Well, surprise, you miniscule bitch." I spit the words into her petite ear. "Did you not realize what you were doing? How close you came to ruining our lives? She looks up dazed, looking like she is ready to slip into a heroin induced dream state, into my shaded brown eyes, still appalled as she recognizes it is me. Too shocked to even open her mouth to scream; I slip the sharp blade into her chest, through the ironed white cotton blouse, exactly into the side ventricles of the heart muscle I had studied so well in Anatomy 101. "This is for you, Sick Sophia. This is for taking my Jerod away." And I shift the knife around. I know exactly where I have it. Christ! The blood! I withdraw it. I pull off my bloodied gloves and shove them and the knife into the bag. For some reason I think of Thanksgiving and pulling turkey gizzards out from the inside. There is that damn word again. Turkey. Why am I thinking about this? I know why. I wish I had taken her heart out. But that is just too hard. I will have to be happy with simply stabbing it. She has, obviously, slumped to the ground. Her mouth is gurgling strange sounds of horror. I pull her further into the murky shadow hoping cruelly that blood is the sound I am hearing. I know this wish so well.

Tempest, if you ever *read* this. Be assured: I had checked this alley out days prior. I knew where the sun would be up in the sky at this time of day. I knew her schedule. I knew her steps. I had it all under control. Then, I squatted and checked her disgusting pulse. None! The world was now a better place. Phew. My last and finest Aries secret was successful.

I pulled my hood tighter, ran straight out the other side of the narrow passage way. I had my knife wrapped in a plastic bag now, beside my gloves, in my pocket. I reach the light of the sidewalk and feel the warmth of the stunning blue New York sky open up above me. I hear her humming, but I don't see her. *Nana. Where are you?* She is humming dad's song.

"Heaven, I'm in heaven."

Running home I take a serious detour toward the Upper West. I am up to it with the adrenaline of a murder pumping through my veins. I am a runner now. I fly with endorphins of power, I jog through Columbus Circle. I run upstairs to the public restroom near the Borders. The long hallway to get there feels like a million blocks. I look around. It is empty. It is early on a Sunday by New York standards. I hurry in and look around. Empty. Phew again. I wash my hands. I take out the plastic bag. I pull out the gloves dropping it into the silver, sleek wastebasket under the sink. Even through the silver and its plastic lining I see them: the bright yellow with blood all over them. They look like flames of yellow and red. Flames of death. I keep the knife wrapped inside my bag and close it tight; I put it back inside my sweatshirt.

I look down into the trash. I pull the bag tight and tie a knot. I look into the mirror. I look the same. I am okay. No regrets. I am actually glowing. A murder glow. I carry the bag out into the long corridor in a non-conspicuous manner. I rush down the escalator and jog toward Hell's Kitchen. Where should I throw my evidence? They always search trash trucks on <u>Law and Order</u>. I have to find another solution. I cannot think of any. I give in. It will have to be. I run down toward the river, suddenly I pause. A trash can is on the pier where one of the ferries is going for a ride around the statue. Surely that trash goes somewhere else. Far away. Maybe across the river? Tourists from Holland are lining up. I throw the bag into the ship's can. A large Turkish man throws a paper coffee cup into the can. His son throws a bag left over from a pretzel. They speak Turkish to one another. I jog back up towards 9th. I duck into The Cupcake Café on 9th and buy a mocha cupcake, a walnut maple one and two chocolate-chocolates. I know what the boys like. Mike, the lovable large owner speaks to me in his poetic haiku way. I like him. He is real. He has no clue to this, my newest secret. He treats me to a Latte and I leave.

Later, laden down with Mike's cupcakes and some onion, egg and sun-dried tomato bagels, I can see that the guys are all up watching baseball in the den, the Mets against the Dodgers. Jeremy had taped it from the night before. "Anyone want a bagel?" Justin hops up to come into the kitchen. Figures. He's hungry already. God, he makes me nuts. I plop the bagels and cream cheese on the counter. He empties the bag and grabs a couple of napkins. He's grabbing orange juice from the fridge. I retreat to the living room. What have I just done? Christ! I killed her.

"Cool. You got onion." He is rustling through the silverware drawer noisily. Ahhhhh! He yells out:

"Where is that sharp small knife, mom? Mom? The one we always use for bagels?"

"Yes, just a moment. I have it. Just let me rinse it off," I whisper, shaking with joy. I had committed murder. But had I snapped? Not a bit. I was saving my family. *I simply did what I had to do.*

The cold tap water was tinged in Sophia's deep red Sicilian blood as it rushes down the silver colored chrome drain around the murder weapon. It was, in point of fact very pleasant to look at; there was a red water color look to it and I reminded myself I must start doing water colors again. Tempest, you like water colors, too; I think I remember you saying that. Coral, indigo, plum red, cherry... I thought of all the cool names of paints now. Of lipstick colors I would still be able to try. I picture her melon lips. I watch as the red gets lighter and lighter, changing to a muted watery coral, then a warm pastel pink, until the water is clear and clean as it rushes for the drain.

"Here it is sweetheart." I hand him the knife. "Be careful, now." He looks at the knife long and hard.

"Mom, did you know this isn't a real bagel knife? The real ones curve down at the end. This is just the one we use, right?" I nod. God, do I love these boys.

A yellow cloud outside the kitchen window begins to spin softly and Nana's humming is heard just as our new day begins. Let me see. Now, what is she humming? Oh I know, "Cheek to Cheek." Was there some wonderful significance to this? "I'm in heaven. And my heart beats so that I can hardly speak. And I seem to find the happiness I seek. When we're out together dancing cheek to cheek." I have been thinking, perhaps it is a good time now to finally change my name for good. Yes. I will start the legal proceedings tomorrow. It is time. What do you think?

Oh, by the way, please remember, Tempest. This was just a dream.

Haven

SMUDGED IN GRAY AND SAGE GREEN NOW

Chapter 35

By: Tempest

First, I need to write to her and reassure her she made the right decision not to kill Sophia. Do you really think anybody can just go out and kill? It is a bit concerning that her dreams and other visions have been so detailed and violent. But, at the same time the stabbing one was easy to follow. You know not only Haven's secret, do you my trusted reader? Now you know my secret, too. Haven does deserve to be called Heaven. Look at what she has been through; and, after all, she didn't murder Sophia.

I am constantly now seeing things, hearing things, feeling things of others. Even others' dreams and visions, like Haven's. She didn't even need to send me such a detailed version of her dream. I had already seen it. These thoughts and visions are becoming more and more blurred with what is going on in my immediate world. I feel distorted between real and unreal, my life and others' lives. The line between right and wrong is now smudged altogether in a dark grayish sage green—a funny blend of Sarah's mint color and Sophia's dark hair. It could get ugly.

Evil has no boundaries for me if it means saving the soul of one of my friends. It always comes around, you see. If you do wrong, it comes back at you. My murder of Creepo caught me in a "wrong"sphere forever. It has come back to envelope me in its ugly arms. Still, I will do whatever it takes to care for my good and trusted friends. Heaven is such a friend. My Aries friend. I sound sane, don't I? I am good at that. Haven (now Heaven) didn't kill Sophia.

I did.

Suong's father stood quietly and watched me. He was far away, in a shadow under an eave with binoculars held up to his eyes. He watched me stab her. It was so very much like his daughter Suong used to do on the hillside behind our house in Portsmouth. He saw me cross over to the other side. I looked up slowly, clad in the Highline sweatshirt matching Heaven's dream, and as I stared at him, I knew that would not be the last time I'd see him. He raised his arm and in his hand he held the patch Suong wore. He swung it around and around like a lasso, it catching the sunlight's particles as he twirled in the air.

I turned and rushed back to our hotel so fast it was like I was an Olympic gold medalist runner. He had scared me to death. When I arrived, Mario was napping. I sat down and took out some stationary from the hotel desk drawer. I was happy to see the Gramercy still had old fashioned stationary in their rooms. I wrote this:

Dear Heaven,

I have spent a lot of time now—reading your journals, speaking with you by phone and examining your plight, all with much contemplation. I am sure there are many layers of life and emotion you haven't shared with me or anyone else, for that matter. Your Aries secrets. I will tell you that if in your heart you believe Jerod loves you, and if you indeed love him, then you are right to give your love to this marriage. As you yourself have said, no one said marriage is easy. It isn't. Neither is forgiveness, but remember that your hurt is probably not as deep as his. I know Jerod broke your heart and shattered a part of you. <u>But he didn't shatter you</u>. You are strong. Your children deserve for you to remain together. That is my advice to you.

I have a strong intuition that Sophia will no longer bother you or your family.

Regarding your theft from the Tariks, Inc. give the money back. You are no thief. You will eventually be discovered and it will ruin the new life you are trying to create.

I hope I have helped in some way. I must move on. There is a twin, a Gemini woman named Hope, who has never met her identical twin sister she has been told her entire life doesn't exist. They have been, for all intensive purposes, nothing but ghosts to one another. "My Gemini Ghost"... perhaps, this next time when I help it will not involve murder.

But, it is what it is, and I will do what I must. For love never fails. It finds its way.

Warmly,

Tempest

TOPICS FOR DISCUSSION QUESTIONS

1. Tempest has changed. Are there any clues to this throughout the book? What are they?

2. Haven decides to forgive Jerod. Do you understand all the complicated reasons why she chose to do this?

3. What is the significance of Haven and her name change? What does this change represent to her?

4. Does Haven's personality show she is Aries?

5. Did you have any clues Amber loves Haven prior to Haven letting us know Amber tells her so while in the cab?

6. The psychic helps Haven discover some truths. Do you believe in this type of fortune telling?

7. What do you think caused Tempest to go from a normal wife who justifiably kills her husband's murderer to a serial killer in support of hurt or damaged women?

8. Tempest says secrets usually come out. Do you agree?

All the latest news about Claudia, her books and her astrology thriller book tour can be found on her blog that is on her website at www.claudiahoagmcgarry.com, *or* you can write to her at Claudia.tempest@me.com. She is available for book club and writing group visits while she is not working on her newest book, *My Gemini Ghost*, about Hope and Joy, the Gemini twin sisters from New Orleans who have never met and do not even know that the other exists. Yet, intuitively, each senses that a deep, dark secret has been kept from her. These two strong women will not give up until they are the *one soul* they were born to be.

Copyright © 2011 Claudia Hoag Mc Garry

All rights reserved.

ISBN:
ISBN-13:

LCCN

CPSIA information can be obtained at www.ICGtesting.com
Printed in the USA
LVOW10s1511041113

359953LV00015B/797/P

9 781463 696290